Edited by Belinda Gallagher

ISBN 0 86112 632 7
Published by Brimax Books Ltd, Newmarket, England 1991.
Printed in Hong Kong.

MY BEDTIME STORYBOOK

Illustrated by Ken Morton

Brimax · Newmarket · England

Contents

Dooley and the Dogwhistle Jellyberries

"Mmm, this tastes good," said Dooley Duck, as he gobbled a big chunk of soggy bread floating in the river.

"But you eat **all** the bread," complained his friends. "You're very greedy."

Dooley just laughed. "I'm not greedy," he said. "I'm just faster than you, that's all."

Some children threw stale cake into the river. And then an old lady threw some broken biscuits. Dooley swam as fast as he could and gobbled everything up.

"But we're hungry," wailed the other ducks.

"Then you'll just have to swim faster," laughed Dooley.

But day by day Dooley began to feel heavier. He still swam faster than the others and gobbled up all the food, but he got fatter and fatter. One day he saw a rather nice wedge of currant cake float by. But he couldn't swim after it. He just sank under the water until only his head was showing.

All the other ducks swam by and laughed. "You'll just have to swim faster, Dooley," they said. "This currant cake is delicious!" But Dooley felt very, very silly. Whoever heard of a duck who was too fat to float!

He decided to go for a walk along the river bank. He soon felt puffed, so he stopped for a rest. He noticed a crooked pink door in the side of the bank. Suddenly the door opened and there stood a funny little man dressed all in blue. "You're the Water Wizard!" cried Dooley.

"I am," said the little man. "I'm in charge of the river. Why aren't you swimming with all the other ducks?"

Dooley felt very silly again. "Because I'm too fat," he mumbled. "My body sinks under the water."

The Water Wizard threw back his head and laughed. "What a joke!" he said. "A duck who is too fat to float!"

Dooley went inside the Water Wizard's home. It was warm and cosy and very soon Dooley couldn't stop yawning. "You can sleep in my laundry basket," said the Water Wizard. Dooley snuggled his tired, heavy body inside and fell asleep in seconds.

The next day he felt much better. "Please could you magic me thin again?" he asked the Water Wizard.

But the Water Wizard shook his head. "You've been very greedy," he said. "You shouldn't have gobbled all that food."

"I know," said Dooley, hanging his head.

The Water Wizard flicked through his Spell Book. "There is one spell I could try," he said. "I need a big bowl of Dogwhistle Jellyberries."

"Dogwhistle Jellyberries?" echoed Dooley.

"Yes," said the Water Wizard. "They are very rare, but if you can pick me a bowlful I will make you thin again *and* I'll make you a big chocolate cake with nuts and cherries."

9

At the mention of chocolate cake with nuts and cherries Dooley grabbed the empty bowl and set off to look for the berries. He saw a large bush covered in black berries. "Are these Dogwhistle Jellyberries?" he muttered to himself.

"No," giggled an otter. "They're blackberries!"

He waddled along the river bank until he saw a bush laden with green berries. "I wonder if these are Dogwhistle Jellyberries," he whispered to himself.

"No, they're not," laughed a rabbit. "They're gooseberries!"

He carried on until he came to a bush of juicy red berries. "Now these must be Dogwhistle Jellyberries," he said. But a squirrel laughed so much he nearly fell out of his tree.

"Dogwhistle Jellyberries!" he said. "Those berries are raspberries!"

Dooley had walked for miles and was feeling very tired but he only had to think of the chocolate cake with nuts and cherries and he waddled a bit faster. But ten days and ten nights later Dooley knocked on the Water Wizard's door. He held out the empty bowl. "I couldn't find any Dogwhistle Jellyberries anywhere," he said.

But the Water Wizard roared with laughter.

"You're not cross?" asked Dooley.

10

"Of course not!" giggled the Water Wizard. "It was a joke! There is no such berry as the Dogwhistle Jellyberry!"

"But I've been walking for ten days and ten nights looking for them!" spluttered Dooley. "You said you'd make me thin again!"

"But I have," said the Water Wizard. "Just look at yourself."

Dooley's fat tummy had disappeared. "It's all that walking," said Dooley. "I'm thin again!" He slid carefully into the water. "And I can float!" he cried.

Then the Water Wizard gave him a huge chocolate cake with nuts and cherries. "Now don't gobble it all at once and get fat again," he said.

"I won't," said Dooley. "Please can I borrow your laundry basket?"

He tied some string to his legs and around the handle of the basket. Then he  put the cake in the basket and swam up the river to his friends, towing the cake behind him.

He gave all his friends a big chunk of cake. "I'm sorry I was so greedy," he said. "It was no fun being so fat and heavy."

"But how did you get thin so quickly?" asked his friends as they munched the soft, gooey cake.

"Well, it's all because of a very rare plant," grinned Dooley. "You won't have heard of it. It's called the Dogwhistle Jellyberry!"

The King of the Beasts

One day, a long time ago, all the animals gathered together to see who should become their king.

"I think I should be king," said the giraffe. "With my tall neck I can see above the trees. I know everything that happens for miles around and a good king should be able to watch over his land."

"That's silly," said the crocodile. "I should be king. With my hundreds of teeth I could bite the head off anyone that disobeys me. A good king should be able to rule over his subjects and keep control. Well, I could do that with my teeth."

"I should be king," said the eagle. "I can fly in the air and see everything for miles and miles. I can see a lot more than the giraffe and my talons are just as good as the crocodile's teeth to keep control."

"I'd make the best king," said the hyena. "I laugh at everything and a good king should have a sense of humour."

"That's ridiculous," said the tiger. "I'm the biggest of all the cats. I should be king. Besides I've got a beautiful coat and kings should be dressed in beautiful things."

"I should be king," said the camel. "I can go for ages and ages without water. None of you can, so I should be king."

"I," said the snake, "can crawl under stones, up trees, swim through water. In fact, I can do almost everything. So I should be king."

"You can't be king," said the rhinoceros, "You don't have any legs. You couldn't run away from your enemies. I, on the other hand, have very strong legs. I'm the biggest animal to walk on land. I should be king."

"Do you mind, cousin," bellowed the elephant. "I happen to be the biggest animal to live on land. You may be second to me, but I'm the biggest and because of that I should be king."

"Hold on just a minute," roared the lion. "We all have different opinions of who should be king and I don't think that we'll agree however long we're here. So I have a plan."

"What is it?" all the animals shouted.

"Let's all vote. The one who gets the most votes can be king."

"Good idea," said all the animals. "Let's vote then."

The ostriches folded up pieces of paper and everyone took one piece. Then the monkeys ran around giving everyone a pen.

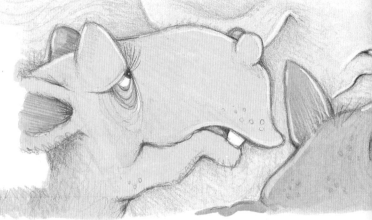

"Just write the name of the animal you wish to be king on the piece of paper with this pen," they said, "Then put it in the box that the gorilla has."

Meanwhile, the lion was mingling amongst the different animals. He went up to the hyena and said, "You'd like to be king, wouldn't you?"

The hyena nodded.

"Well then," said the lion, "If you vote for me. I'll vote for you."

The hyena nodded. "Thank you, lion, I'll certainly vote for you."

One by one, the lion went up to the other animals and told them all the same thing. So when each animal voted, they voted for the lion, thinking he was going to vote for them. When the last piece of paper was in the box the baboons emptied it and counted out the votes. Then the eldest baboon stood up and said, "The winner is the lion!"

All the animals were disappointed, except the lion. 'But,' they all thought, 'At least he voted for me, so he will make a good king after all.'

And to this day the lion is still the King of the Beasts.

13

Herbert and the Wontawongas

There was once a young dragon called Herbert who lived in an old, abandoned castle with his parents and sister. One day Herbert caught a terrible cold and had to stay in bed for a week. When at last Herbert got better he found he could no longer breathe fire. Herbert was very upset because a dragon who can't breathe fire isn't really a dragon at all.

Herbert went to talk to his father.

"I can't breathe fire like a real dragon any more," said Herbert.

"Then you must practice breathing fire every morning for ten minutes," said his father.

So Herbert started practising fire-drill every morning, but nothing happened except that his throat got very red and sore. His sister Millicent gave Herbert a scarf to wrap around his sore throat.

"Wear this, Herbert," she said. "You must get your fire back."

One day Herbert left the castle for a breath of fresh air. He wanted to take his mind off his sore throat. He was walking through a nearby wood when suddenly he came face to face with a wontawonga.

Now the wontawongas are the natural enemies of dragons. Wontawongas can't breathe fire like dragons. Instead, they overcome their enemies by breathing out a very bad smell.

Herbert stopped dead in his tracks.

"A dragon!" said the wontawonga. "What are you doing here? This wood belongs to the wontawongas."

"I thought the wood belonged to everyone," said Herbert.

"You're wrong," said the wontawonga. "You are trespassing."

"Trespassing?" said Herbert. "I didn't see a 'NO TRESPASSING' sign."

"That's because it blew down in the storm last night," said the Wontawonga, whose name was Frithle.

"There wasn't a storm last night," said Herbert. "I know because I stood at my window all last night wishing I could breathe fire again like a real dragon."

"Oh, so you don't know how to breathe fire any more?" said Frithle, his eyes bulging with surprise.

Herbert went very red.

'I should never have given my secret away to a wontawonga,' he thought to himself.

"Come with me!" ordered Frithle. "And if you don't . . . I'll breathe on you!"

So Herbert reluctantly trudged after Frithle the wontawonga. As they walked through the wood the light began to fade and the trees seemed to grow bigger and taller.

'I wonder what wontawongas eat?' thought Herbert, who was starting to get rather hungry.

After walking a long way Herbert saw a light ahead, though rather a dim sort of light, and then they came out of the wood and onto the edge of a muddy bank.

Frithle threw back his head and let out a strange cry, a bit like the sound of water being sucked down a pipe, only ten times louder. Out of the pond crawled several larger, even uglier versions of Frithle.

"There's Uncle Gazump!" yelled Frithle. "And Aunt Mergatrude!" And then he coughed slightly and said, "This is Herbert the dragon. I captured him."

"You did nothing of the sort," said Herbert. "I must go home now, you know. Dinner's at seven."

The three wontawongas all burst out laughing.

"Go home?" said Gazump. "Ha, ha, what an idea."

"I must go home," said Herbert. "We're having roast chicken, roast potatoes, peas and gravy."

"Chicken, potatoes, peas and gravy!" the three wontawongas shouted, shaking with laughter again. "We can offer you something even better. Fricasee of lizard liver and toad-in-the-hole with real toad!"

Real toad! Herbert was disgusted.

Just as he was beginning to despair of ever getting home for dinner, Herbert had an idea. He waited for the right moment to try it out.

The right moment came when the wontawongas had gathered round their dinner table, a flat slab of rock lying on the ground.

"Have a lizard!" shouted Frithle.

"Er . . . in a moment," said Herbert, hoping that if he waited the wontawongas would eat up all the lizards. When they were about to start on the toads Herbert decided to try out an idea.

"Have you ever tried cooking your food?" he asked.

"Cooking our food?" roared Gazump. "What a ridiculous idea!"

"Well, we always cook our food," said Herbert. "It brings out the flavour. Look, I'll show you." He picked up one of the toads, and started to blow on it. With each blow his fiery dragon's breath got a little bit stronger and a little bit hotter.

"Here, have a taste," said Herbert, and he handed over the roast toad to Gazump, the oldest wontawonga. Gazump put the toad in his mouth and began to chew.

"Delicious!" he boomed. So Herbert quickly roasted a round of toads. The Wontawongas were so busy stuffing themselves with the roasted toads that they didn't notice how fiery and hot Herbert's breath was becoming.

It was starting to get dark and cold.

"Would you like me to make a fire?" asked Herbert.

"A fire?" said Mergatrude. "We've never had a fire. All right, make us a fire."

So Herbert started to look around for bits of wood, and when he had got a big pile ready he started to breathe on it. Soon it became a great big bonfire.

A few miles away, Herbert's mother and father were standing on top of their castle wall, wondering what had happened to Herbert. After a while they saw the flames in the middle of the wontawonga wood.

"I think that fire must have been started by Herbert," said Herbert's father. "The wontawongas don't know how to make fire. Herbert must be in trouble."

"Why don't we send out the grettyhounds?" said Herbert's mother. The grettyhounds were five times larger than greyhounds, and a pack of them was kept at the castle. So Herbert's father ordered the grettyhounds to go and look for Herbert in the wood.

Meanwhile, the wontawongas stood around Herbert's huge bonfire, unable to take their eyes off the brightly burning wood. When the grettyhounds burst upon the scene the wontawongas were taken completely by surprise. They rushed away, crashing through the trees, with the grettyhounds nipping at their heels.

Later that evening, safe at home again, Herbert told his family about his adventure.

"I was lucky to get my dragon breath back just in time," said Herbert.

Then a few moments later he added, "You know it's the most amazing thing, but roast toad tastes exactly like chicken!"

19

The Tale of Samuel Figg

On the very top of Windy Hill,
Stood scarecrow, Samuel Figg.
He had a turnip head,
And a suit of red,
And a hat that was far too big.

One day the wind blew very strong,
Sam wobbled and he swayed.
"Oh heavens!" he said,
As he felt his bald head,
And his hat fluttered off and away.

It twirled across the fields of corn,
To a tree where it caught on a twig.
But it knocked down a nest,
Mrs Wren was distressed,
"Just look what you've done, Samuel Figg!"

"What will I do? Where will I sleep?
For I'll lay my eggs in a while."
"Don't worry," Sam said,
"Have my hat instead."
Mrs Wren climbed inside with a smile.

But standing on top of Windy Hill,
Sam's head felt cold and bare.
"I feel silly," he said,
"With a bald turnip head,
I'll knit a new hat," he declared.

So with sticks and string he got busy,
But his knitting was no good at all.
He got tangled in string,
Without knitting a thing,
And he rolled down the hill like a ball.

Mrs Wren went to help poor old Sam,
She pecked all the string into shreds.
Then she twittered and sang,
"I've a wonderful plan!"
And she stuck bits of string to Sam's head!

Soon Sam's head was covered in string.
And arranged in a nice curly style.
And Samuel Figg,
In his rather nice wig,
Was the best looking scarecrow for miles!

The Bogle and the Bear

Once upon a time there was a miller. He lived in a fine windmill with four huge sails and although he lived by himself, he was happy. The people who brought their corn to be made into flour talked to him and told him all the news of the village so he never felt lonely. When the day was done and the long evening shadows crept across the fields, he would sigh contentedly and admire the neat sacks of flour that showed he had done a good day's work. Then he enjoyed his own company; he lit his pipe and put his feet up to sit and dream happy dreams.

This was an ideal life until the dreadful day that a bogle decided to come and live at the mill with the miller.

Bogles are a nuisance. They are little goblins who take up residence unasked and unwanted. They are full of mischief, and if ever anything is lost and cannot be found, it's more than likely that a bogle has taken it. If a room that is left nice and tidy is a swirling muddle ten minutes later, it is almost certain that a bogle has done the mischief. The trouble is that once a bogle has decided to settle anywhere, it is very hard to get rid of it. No amount of asking nicely does any good, no amount of scolding is any use. The bogle has to decide for himself that he is going to leave.

The first the miller knew of the bogle in the mill was one fine morning when a brisk wind was blowing and the sails of the windmill refused to go round. He hurried outside to find out what was wrong and saw a horrid little goblin dressed in green with pointed ears and a mischievous grin on his face, clinging to one of the sails.

"Let go of that sail!" cried the miller angrily.

"Shan't!" said the bogle.

"Then I'll make you," said the miller, picking up a big stick.

The bogle grinned with glee. This was the kind of game he liked best, making people angry and outwitting them. The miller couldn't shift the bogle who was as slippery as an eel and as cunning as a fox. The miller lost a morning's work until the bogle tired of his game.

23

The next thing the miller knew of the bogle was when he picked up a sack of flour to load it onto a customer's cart. He pulled the sack onto his shoulder and as he did so, the flour began to run out in a stream from the slit the bogle had made in the bottom of the sack. The miller was furious at the lost flour and at the mess on his clean floor, there were floury footprints everywhere. What was worse was that the bogle kept just out of his reach and laughed in a mocking way that drove the miller mad.

That evening, when his work was finished, instead of sitting happily with his feet up dreaming, the miller stomped off to the village to talk over his troubles with his friends. As he drank his ale in the tavern, he told his tale to an interested but slightly disbelieving audience. "It's as true as I'm sitting here," he told them indignantly.

"It certainly is," said old Percy who had seen the bogle at work for himself.

On the edge of the group of listeners was a stranger dressed in brightly coloured clothes with gold earrings in his ears. After a while, he came up to the miller and said, "If I get rid of the bogle for you, will you give me a gold piece?"

The miller drew in his breath sharply. A gold piece! That was a lot of money. He wondered how many days milling it would take him to earn that much, it would take him a long time. But then he thought of the bogle. No matter how hard the miller worked, he wouldn't make much money at all if it stayed in the mill, stopping the sails and spilling the flour. And goodness knows what mischief the bogle might think up for tomorrow.

"Done!" cried the miller. "Get rid of that bogle and you shall have a gold piece as sure as I'm sitting here."

"Come with me, then," said the man. He took the miller out to the stables behind the tavern and called softly, "Bryony." There was a shifting in the straw, a sleepy grumbling, rumbling sound and a big, brown bear came shuffling over to the door.

"This is my dearest friend, Bryony," said the man, reaching up to rub the bear's ears. "He's very friendly to those I like, but woe betide those who get on the wrong side of me."

The miller stepped back nervously and said, "Tell him I'm a friend."

The man laughed and did so and they all set off, in the moonlight, to the mill.

When they got there the man whispered a few words into the bear's ear and opened the door and let him in.

"It's best if we wait out here," he told the miller who was only too pleased to stay outside if there was to be a fight.

26

There was a rumbling and a grumbling, a growling and a howling, a bumping and a thumping when all of a sudden, the door burst open and the bogle came shooting out like a bullet with the snarling bear not far behind him.

"I'm off," cried the bogle. "I don't like your mill after all." And he ran down the road as fast as his green-shod feet would carry him.

The man soon calmed the bear who the miller rewarded with a pot of his best honey. He gladly handed over a gold piece to the bear's master. He and the bear spent the night in the miller's shed, tucked up in some clean straw and next day they set off on their travels again.

The miller's life got back to normal as soon as he had cleared up the muddle the bogle had left. Once more he spent his days working happily and his evenings dreaming quietly.

One winter's evening as the miller sat enjoying the warmth of his fire, the door opened a crack and to his dismay he saw the bogle peering in. This time the bogle wasn't grinning, he was looking anxious.

"I was thinking of coming back here," he said. "Have you still got that big brown cat?"

For a moment the miller was puzzled, then he realised the bogle meant the bear. He thought quickly. "Indeed I have," he said. "She's out at the back at the moment, feeding her seven kittens. Lovely they are and growing quite big now . . ."

But the bogle had gone. The thought of that rumbling and grumbling, bumping and thumping multiplied seven times was too much for him and the miller never saw him again.

What Happened to the Twelfth Roll?

Long, long ago when ladies wore crinolines and gentlemen wore top hats and boys and girls bowled hoops and whipped their spinning tops, a clever dog called Bess lived with a large family in London. Bess was a very pretty spaniel who was nearly all white except for brown tips to her ears and tiny brown spots along her back, like freckles.

Bess was very happy. She played with the children in the nursery and in the garden, she went for walks with them in the park. She rode in the carriage at Mrs Brown's feet when she drove out to call on her friends and she watched Cook while she made pies, puddings and cakes.

Bess was so clever that she could do tricks. She could sit up and beg, she could roll over and 'die for her country', she could shake a paw with visitors and she could go shopping.

Every morning before breakfast, Cook got out a light shopping basket and called Bess. Bess would come running, her eyes bright and her ears flying and, taking the basket by the handle, she would set out for the baker's shop.

Down the road where the Browns lived she would trot sedately, carefully carrying the basket. Round the corner Bess would go, taking no notice if someone said, "What a clever dog!" or, "Here, girl, show me what you've got in your basket." Along the next street she would go until she came to the baker's shop.

Plump Mrs Smiggens, the baker's wife served behind the counter. "Good morning, Bess," she would say. "Come for the breakfast rolls, have you?"

Bess would put down the basket and sit patiently while Mrs Smiggens counted out twelve warm, newly baked rolls. She would wrap them in a clean checked napkin then give Bess the basket.

More slowly now, being careful not to drop the basket, Bess would go back along the street, round the corner and into the Browns' road, proudly carrying the family's breakfast.

When she got back to the house, Cook would take the basket, put the rolls on the dish for the maid to take into the dining room. Then Cook would pat Bess, tell her what a good dog she was and give her a biscuit.

Rain or shine, hail or snow, every morning, Bess fetched the twelve rolls for the Browns' breakfast.

One morning, after breakfast, Cook knocked on the dining room door and asked to see Mrs Brown.

"What is it, Cook?"

"Sorry to trouble you, Ma'am, but Bess only brought eleven rolls home this morning."

"Oh dear," said Mrs Brown. "I'll speak to the baker."

But when she went to the baker's shop, Mrs Smiggens told Mrs Brown that Bess had been given twelve rolls.

Next day Cook came to Mrs Brown with the same complaint. Again Mrs Brown went to the baker's shop. Mrs Smiggens put her hand on her heart and swore that Bess had been given twelve rolls.

What had happened to the twelfth roll? Surely Mrs Smiggens wasn't cheating. Surely Bess couldn't have eaten the roll on her way home.

Jack, the eldest of Mrs Brown's six children said, "Tomorrow when Bess goes to the bakers, I shall follow her."

Next morning, when Bess left the house carefully carrying the basket with the clean napkin in it, Jack followed a little way behind, dodging from gateway to gateway so the dog couldn't see him.

When Bess went into the bakers as usual, Jack watched through the window. He counted with Mrs Smiggens as she put the rolls in, ten, eleven, twelve.

As Bess came out with her laden basket, he followed her down the street, round the corner and into their road. At the third house along, Bess stopped and put down the basket.

Jack watched as she carefully drew back the napkin and delicately lifted the top roll out. 'Aha!' he thought. 'This is where she eats a secret breakfast.'

But Jack was wrong. Bess pushed open the gate and slipped into the garden where there was a big dog kennel. Bess went up to it and Jack saw to his surprise that Bess laid down the roll which was quickly taken by another dog. It was a thin, bedraggled mother dog with four, squeaky puppies.

As soon as Bess had fed her friend, she came back to the basket, pulled the napkin over the remaining rolls, carried them home and handed them over to Cook. When Jack explained to his mother what she had seen, she understood. The people living across the street were away so the mother dog was not being fed and was too good a mother to leave her puppies while she searched for food. Bess had taken pity on her and was giving her a roll every morning.

After breakfast, Mrs Brown sent Jack to see Mrs Smiggens.

"Tell her she can give Bess thirteen rolls every day until the people across the street come home, and ask Cook for a bowl of scraps for the mother dog."

So Bess was able to go on doing her good deed every day.

Billy's Dressing Gown

When Billy opened the parcel from his mother and father on his birthday and saw that the present was a dressing-gown, he was a little disappointed.
As soon as he saw the box, he knew it wouldn't be the toy car he wanted, it was quite the wrong shape. He said thank you as politely as he could because he did not want to hurt their feelings. He turned to his other parcels and opened them. There were some nice things, but no-one had bought him the car he so badly wanted.

Once he got over his disappointment, Billy enjoyed his birthday. His mother took him to the zoo and he rode on an elephant and fed the sea-lions. His father came home early to watch Billy blow out the candles on his cake. As he blew the candles out, Billy wished a special wish about the car.

Soon after that, it was time to get ready for bed. Billy put on his new dressing-gown over his pyjamas. It was made of soft wool and felt warm and cosy. It was his favourite colour, blue as a summer sky. Really, if he had wanted a dressing-gown and not a pedal car, it was just what he would have chosen. What Billy did not know, was that it was a very special dressing-gown.

As he trotted along the passage to the bathroom to wash, he played his usual pretending game of getting there a different way.

"I'm driving a car," he said and suddenly, he was! He wasn't just turning an imaginary wheel and going brrm, brrm, he was sitting behind the wheel of a red pedal car just like the one he had wished for. Billy was so surprised, he could hardly believe it. When he got to the end of the passage, he shouted, "Stop!" and found himself standing outside the bathroom door. The pedal car had gone as mysteriously as it had come.

Billy turned round and tried again. "I'm riding a bicycle," he said.

No sooner had he said the words than he was riding a shiny two-wheeler like the one that belonged to the boy next door. When he cried, "Stop!" the bicycle disappeared.

Billy was shaking with excitement. Why could he suddenly do magic? Was it because he was a year older today? It couldn't be that, he had several friends older than him and they couldn't do magic. Could it be the dressing-gown? There was only one way to find out. With trembling fingers, he untied the cord and took it off.

"I'm flying a helicopter," he said firmly. Nothing happened.

He snatched up the dressing-gown and put it on again. "I'm flying a helicopter," he repeated.

Instantly, he heard the whirr of the rotary blades. He was in a boy-sized helicopter rising into the air. "Stop," he called and found himself standing outside the bathroom door.

His mother's voice floated up the stairs. "Don't forget to clean your teeth. I'll be up in a minute to tuck you in."

Quickly, Billy brushed his teeth. He tried to decide how to travel back to the bedroom.

"I'm riding an elephant," he said daringly. Suddenly he was swaying along, sitting astride a great, grey neck with two flapping ears on either side and a swishing trunk before him. At the bedroom door he said, "Stop," and the elephant vanished.

When his mother came up, Billy was sitting up in bed. "You were noisy tonight," she said. "It sounded like a herd of elephants stomping along the passage."

Billy laughed delightedly and threw his arms round her neck. "Thank you for the dressing-gown," he said. "It's the best present ever."

His mother was surprised. "I'm glad you like it. I was afraid you were sad because you didn't have a car. We couldn't afford a car *and* a dressing-gown and you needed a new one so much. The man in the shop said it was very special. It was the only one like it and the little boy who got it would be very pleased. You certainly seem to be."

"It's great," said Billy. "Better than a car."

Billy's mother tucked him up and put out the light. After she had gone, Billy put his hand on the dressing-gown to make sure it didn't fly away. He fell asleep thinking happily of all the ways he would be able to travel now he had a magic dressing-gown.

The Green and Hairy Bicycle

Right at the bottom of Toomey Lane there is a haunted castle. It has an iron gate, big dark windows and a flagpole without a flag. Inside the castle lives a young ghost called Miranda Boo.

One day Miranda Boo asked her mother if she could go out to play with the other children in Toomey Lane.

"Certainly not," said her mother. "Ghosts are meant to play with other ghosts, not with children."

"But there aren't any other ghosts on the street," cried Miranda. "I have no one to play with."

"There's the phantom boy in the baker shop," said Mum.

"He's over three hundred years old," said Miranda. "He doesn't know any games."

She sighed sadly and looked out of the window. Across the street she could see a little park. It had trees and swings. Children were buying ice-creams from a van by the fountain.

"Can't I go out for just a little while?" Miranda Boo pleaded again.

"No you can't," said Mum crossly. "And that's that."

Next day Miranda Boo saw a boy called John playing with his brand new bike in the garden next to hers.

"I'd love to have a go on that," said Miranda Boo to herself. "Maybe if I ask John nicely, he'd let me."

When Mum was asleep Miranda Boo floated out of the window and flew to John's garden.

"Hello John," she whispered.

John couldn't see Miranda. He thought her voice was the rustling of the wind in the trees.

'It's useless,' thought Miranda Boo unhappily. 'He'll only see me in the dark.'

She went back to the castle and waited for nightfall. When the sun set, John put his bike away and went indoors for his supper.

Miranda Boo watched sadly. "I'll never have the chance to ride a bike," she wailed.

At midnight there was a knock on the castle door.

"It must be Uncle Dread from America," said Mum happily.

Uncle Dread floated in through the castle wall. He was a very rich ghost and held his head under his right arm.

"I've brought you a present," Uncle Dread said to Miranda Boo.

Miranda Boo opened the parcel. Inside it was a live tarantula.

"It comes in very handy when you want to frighten little children," Uncle smiled.

Miranda Boo dropped the spider on the floor. "I don't want to frighten children," she shouted. "I want to share their bikes."

Uncle Dread looked at the little ghost sternly. "You can't," he said. "The children won't play with you."

"They will!" shouted Miranda Boo, stamping her foot crossly. "All I have to do is ask them in the dark."

Uncle Dread sighed. "Never mind," he said to Mum. "She'll get over it when she makes some ghost friends."

A week after Uncle Dread's visit Miranda Boo was floating above a tree in the park. She heard John talking to a friend.

"Are you going to the fair on Sunday?" said John.

"Of course," replied the friend. "Mum says I could go on the ghost train this year."

Ghost train? Miranda Boo pricked up her ears.

"I'm going on it too," said John. "I'm not scared of the dark."

Miranda hurried back home to the castle. At last she had a plan. She would build her own bicycle and ride it in the tunnel in the ghost train. John and the other children would see her then. They would all find out how good she was at riding bikes and playing games. They'd make friends with her.

Miranda slipped down to the castle's dungeons and rummaged around in the rubbish. She found two rusted iron hoops, an old skeleton and pieces of old metal machinery.

She fixed everything together with nuts and bolts and glue. Then she looked around for more things so that she could ride the bike properly.

Mum was not allowed to come down into the dungeons.

When the bike was finished, Miranda painted it with green dragon's blood and decorated it with wizard's hair.

'Now I've got a green and hairy bicycle,' thought Miranda proudly. 'I bet none of the other children have got such a weird bike.'

Sunday was a hot day. People queued outside the fairground to buy tickets while the band played happy music.

Miranda Boo carried her bike to the ghost-train. It was dark inside the tunnel and the cardboard ghosts looked very real.

Miranda Boo felt a bit scared herself.

The fair opened and the children rushed to the ghost train. Boys and girls clambered onto the seats.

"Hold on tight," the ticket seller said. "We're going in."

With a hoot and a toot, the train rushed into the tunnel. John was sitting in the front car.

"Hello," Miranda Boo said.

"Hello," laughed John. "Are you a cardboard ghost or a bed sheet?"

"I'm a real ghost, you clump," said Miranda.

John laughed again and booed. "There's no such thing as a real ghost," he said. "You're just a pile of sticks and paint."

Miranda felt very angry. Were all children so rude? If they were, she did not want to share her bike with them.

Suddenly there were loud screams. The ghost train lurched. All the other ghosts were moving. "You're not cardboard ghosts at all," shouted Miranda Boo. "You're real."

"Of course we're real," said one of the ghosts. "We all come to the fair every Sunday to race our bikes. Do you want to have a go?"

"You bet I do," shrieked Miranda happily. "I've been looking for friends all over the place."

The race began. Miranda Boo pedalled as fast as she could but the other ghosts were faster still. Miranda Boo finished second from last.

"Never mind," said the champion ghost. "We've had more training than you. Now come on – we've got to play with the kids, otherwise they'll be very disappointed with the ride."

Miranda Boo followed her new-found friends to the train. She sat in the front car next to a girl and wiggled her ears at her.

"You're almost scary," said the girl. "I'm glad I have all my friends with me."

"So am I," said Miranda Boo, flapping her arms like pillow cases. "So am I."

Clarence and the River Pirates

The little alligator King, Clarence, loved to sit in the Royal Tower and watch the boats going up and down the river.

The Tower was so high, Clarence could see all of Alligonia. It was his way of making sure all was well along this part of the river.

Today there was a strange looking ship coming up the river and it made Clarence begin to worry.

Through his royal telescope Clarence could see cannons on the ship's deck. There was a flag flying from the highest mast. His father, Trepador, had told him about flags like this so he knew there was good reason to worry. A black flag with a skull and cross-bones could only mean one thing. A Pirate Ship!

Already the pirates had begun firing their cannons. Clarence had to do something fast!

"Father! Father! FATHER!" he yelled while running down the tower stairs. "Pirates! There are pirates attacking us!"

Trepador had been napping in the sun, but soon came running when he heard how upset his son was.

"Clarence, not so fast," his father said. "Did you say pirates?"

"Yes, yes! And they're attacking the ships on the river. If we don't do something quickly they'll be on land and destroy everything!"

Clarence was running around in little circles and biting his tail, nervously.

"We can't fight back. Our army is too small and too old!" his father said.

"Yes, the army – call the army!" Clarence said. "It's better than doing nothing at all."

Sadly, the Royal Army were far from useful. They were a pack of old and tired hyenas. They had been brave and strong long ago but now they could hardly smile, let alone laugh.

"Just look at them, Clarence," Trepador said, pointing out the window. "They have all seen better days. This is a peaceful kingdom and hasn't needed a real army since The Furious War. And that was a long time ago."

Swagg and Bragg, Clarence's brothers, came running in, shouting and bumping into things.

"Clarence! Father! There are pirates coming to invade us. You have to do something!"

The River Palace was filling up with others who had either seen the pirate ship or heard their cannons. They were all shouting at the little alligator King to do something.

"Yes, I know!" Clarence said. "But what can I do? We have no way to stop them. Stay inside everyone, I'll think of something."

The pirate ship set anchor off shore and the pirate captain stepped down the gang-plank. It was Captain Spitt. A mean and nasty wild boar with a wooden leg and a heart of stone.

"Arrgh! Come on, men, and help yourselves to any loot!" he said. "Go on, take what you want. It's all free today! Ha, ha!"

Captain Spitt was rotten through and through. He thought the animals of Alligonia were hiding because they were frightened.

"Clarence," his father said. "If we make this seem like a really horrible place, the pirates wouldn't want it and they might go away."

44

"How, Father?" Clarence asked. "This kingdom is the most beautiful on all the river and we haven't time to make it look ugly."

"Ahhh, but what if we were all ugly and disgusting? What if we all had something catching? What if we all looked like we had jungle measles?"

"Father, you are brilliant!" Clarence said. "Swagg and Bragg, take some servants and go and fetch that yellow paint we were going to use for the Palace. Father, you call the Royal Painter and tell him to bring all of his brushes."

Jungle measles are very rare. But if you catch them, you become covered in yellow spots and get a tummy ache. That's why people with jungle measles are always moaning.

By the time everyone had enough paint and brushes, Captain Spitt was at the Palace door. His crew of pirate beasts were right behind him!

"Open the door or I'll knock it down with my own two fists! Come on you landlubbers! It's Captain Spitt, the meanest pirate on all the river!"

Actually, he was the only pirate on the river, and not a very clever one at that. Because Alligonia was such a peaceful place, the Palace doors didn't have locks on them. Captain Spitt could have just turned the door knob, but he never thought of that.

Within the Palace, everyone was busy painting spots on each other and practising their moans.

"Hurry up, he could come through the door any minute now!" Clarence said.

"I've nearly finished," said Bragg.

"And me," said Swagg.

At last, everyone had been painted with pretend jungle measles.

"Ready, steady, start moaning!" Clarence said.

"Ohhh! Ohhh! Ohhh!" they moaned and groaned.

"Ha! Ha! Just listen to them, men. They're frightened to bits!" Captain Spitt said.

"You are the rottenest, ugliest, meanest pirate in all the world!" his First Mate answered. "And they all know it. That's why they're so scared."

"Thanks, Matey," said Captain Spitt. "You say the nicest things. Come on men, break down the door!"

They didn't need to. It just swung open. There stood Clarence, his brothers, father and all the animals of Alligonia, covered in great yellow spots, holding their tummies and moaning.

"What's wrong with you lot? Well? Speak up or I'll make you sorry!" the Captain yelled.

"Jungle measles," Clarence whispered.

"What? Speak up!"

"Jungle measles!" Clarence said, much louder this time.

Then Captain Spitt looked all around him. Everyone was covered in spots. Then he looked for his men. They were all running away, back to the ship.

"Oh, oh," Captain Spitt said. And then he fainted.

Clarence quickly painted yellow spots on him, too, which was tricky because he was laughing so much he could barely keep the paint brush steady.

"This will teach him to attack Alligonia!" Clarence said. And they rolled Captain Spitt out of the door.

Captain Spitt woke up and saw his hands and feet were all spotty. He ran for his ship.

"Wait, men! Wait for me! I'm your Captain, remember!"

When the other pirates saw their Captain had jungle measles they made him ride in a tiny boat while the big ship pulled it along.

Poor Captain Spitt. He was so stupid that when the painted-on jungle measles washed off, he thought he had got better! His men let him back on the ship but they never went back to Alligonia.

"The River Palace won't get painted this year, Clarence," Trepador said.

"That's alright," he answered. "I like it just the way it is, don't you?"

Everyone had to agree with their little King, Clarence.

Stripey the Magic Horse

However hard she tried, Lisa could not sleep when she went to bed at night.

"That will never do," said Mrs. Evans who lived next door and she made Lisa a herb pillow.

"It works like magic," she assured Lisa's worried mother. "You'll sleep well now, Lisa," said Mrs. Evans, as she gave Lisa the pillow, which was in the shape of a toy horse. The horse was made from orange and brown striped material with looped brown wool for the mane and tail.

Lisa thanked Mrs. Evans. "I will call my little horse Stripey," she said.

That night Lisa was tucked up in bed reading a book of bedtime stories with Stripey beside her. Lisa was beginning to feel very drowsy, when she felt a movement at her elbow. Stripey was there, pawing the bedclothes with a front hoof.

"Come along Lisa, get on my back. We have a long way to travel tonight," neighed the little horse.

"But I'm too big," Lisa protested sleepily.

"Nonsense!" Stripey snorted. "Just climb on and we'll be off on our first adventure."

Lisa did as she was told and before she knew what was happening, they had jumped right into the picture in her book.

48

As Lisa and Stripey galloped towards the castle in the picture, Lisa saw lots of nursery rhyme and fairy tale people. First there was a little boy dressed in blue, sleeping beside the haystack. Of course! He was Little Boy Blue who should have been looking after the sheep, not to mention the cows in the cornfield.

Then they passed the Old Woman cleaning the windows of The Shoe. When Lisa and Stripey galloped by, a stream of children came pouring out of The Shoe to wave to them. 'No wonder the poor Old Woman never knows what to do,' thought Lisa.

Further down the road they met the Three Bears walking in single file. Great big Father Bear led the way followed by Mother Bear and Baby Bear trailing behind. The Three Bears did not look at all fierce, in fact, they looked exactly like the teddy bears who sat on the shelf in Lisa's bedroom at home.

The castle was very close now. Lisa wondered who lived there, but she did not have time to guess as coming towards them was Bo-Peep. Lisa recognised her as she was carrying a shepherd's crook and crying miserably.

"Have you seen my sheep? I've lost them," sobbed Bo-Peep as Lisa pleaded

with Stripey to stop. "I've looked everywhere for them."

"Leave them alone," Lisa advised, "and they'll come home, bringing their tails behind them."

"Are you sure they will?" asked Bo-Peep, quickly drying her eyes.

"Yes. My picture-book says so," Lisa assured her.

"Oh, thank you, Lisa. I'll go home right away and wait for them there." Bo-Peep smiled happily as she waved good-bye.

At last they reached the castle only to find it was surrounded by a thick, prickly forest.

"Oh dear," wailed Lisa. "However shall we get in?"

"You forget I am a magic horse," snorted Stripey. "If you follow me I will make a pathway through the thorns."

Sure enough the bushes and trees bent away in front of Stripey so that they walked through without even a scratch. Then they passed under a great archway and into the courtyard beyond.

"This is as far as I can go," neighed Stripey. "Now you must go on by yourself."

Fearfully Lisa went into the silent castle. She noticed the pigeons were asleep in the dove-cote and the dogs and cats slept on their satin cushions. Servants were fast asleep where they stood, some still carrying trays of food, others with dusters and mops. Even the King and Queen were asleep on their thrones as Lisa tip-toed by, although she was sure the King would never hear her as he was snoring so loudly.

As she climbed the twisting stairs Lisa could hear a spinning wheel whirring. Someone was awake. Following the sound, Lisa entered a room to find Mrs. Evans busily spinning Baa-Baa Black Sheep's wool. She beckoned to Lisa to try her hand at spinning.

As she sat at the wheel, Lisa felt something prick her finger.

Mrs. Evans smiled. "You'll sleep well now, Lisa," she said.

Frightened, Lisa jumped up and ran into another room, which to her surprise, was exactly like her bedroom at home. She sank down onto her own little bed as she suddenly felt so very sleepy, but just before she closed her eyes she wondered if Prince Charming would come and wake her . . .

The next thing she knew, someone was saying, "Wake up, wake up, Sleeping Beauty."

Lisa opened her eyes to see her Father opening the curtains of her bedroom. The sun shining in through the window made her blink. Was it morning already?

She looked at her pillow, Stripey was lying there as if he had never moved all night. Her bed-time story book still lay open at the picture of the fairy-tale castle of Sleeping Beauty, its tall turrets showing in the distance above a forest of trees.

Had her ride to the castle been just a lovely dream? Lisa felt quite disappointed . . . until she distinctly saw Stripey wink one eye.

51

The Newt and the Frog

A Newt and a Frog, side by side on a log,
Down by the bank of a river.
Argued and quarrelled from morning to night,
As to which of them was the best diver.

"Watch," said the Frog. "I can dive from this log,
A perfection of grace and of style."
"Pah," scoffed the Newt. "You ugly fat brute,
You, graceful! Don't make me smile."

"Take that," cried the Frog, springing up from the log,
And punching the Newt in the eye.
The Newt turned about, and the Frog he did clout,
Just as a Duck waddled by.

She looked at the Newt and the Frog on the log
With a sharp little gleam in her eye.
"Whatever's the matter with you two?" she asked.
So they told her what happened, and why.

"You must have a contest," the wiley Duck quacked.
"And just to make sure it is fair,
I'll be the judge, and then at the end
The winner I will declare."

"A splendid idea," cried the quarrelsome pair.
"Then we shall know who is best."
"Hurry," the Duck quacked impatiently.
"Let us get on with the test."

Straight from the log dived that silly pair,
Both being weak in the head.
With one snap of her beak the Duck caught them neat,
Declaring them equal, though dead!

A Question for the Oggamagog

The big house at the end of the street had been empty for some time. The Oggamagog sat in a dark corner of the basement. The moon was shining through the window. He felt less lonely when the moon was out. He had been in the house, alone, for a long time now. He wished someone would move in soon, so that at least he could hear voices and the sound of footsteps. But it was such a big house, with so many rooms, that nobody seemed to want it. The Oggamagog wondered what would become of him if someone decided to pull the house down.

"You will stay on earth until you have made up for your wickedness," the Great Oggamagog had said. The Oggamagog wondered how long that would be. The Great Oggamagog had been very angry.

One bright December day the Oggamagog was woken by the sound of footsteps coming up the garden path, and then he heard voices.

'At last!' he thought. 'Someone has come to live in the house.'

He heard footsteps passing from room to room. There were shouts, doors banged, and much laughter. The back door opened and he saw some children run into the garden.

The Oggamagog was in the habit of chanting. That night, when he thought everyone was asleep, he began to chant softly.

"O-manna-manna-moon! O manna-manna-moon!" It was a very mournful sound, but nobody heard it. At least not at first. But Stephen Bond wasn't sleeping soundly in his new bed, and eventually he heard the strange sound.

"It must be a ghost!" he said to himself, and he quickly wriggled back under the bedclothes. 'It's too dark to investigate now,' he thought. 'I'll tell Annie about it in the morning.'

Annie, Stephen's sister, didn't believe him when he told her.

"I'm sure it came from the basement," said Stephen. "Let's go and look right now!" So they crept down into the basement, which was rather dark and chilly. There were four rooms and a large hallway. They tiptoed into each room, but they were all empty.

"I'm sure the sound came from down here," said Stephen. "Listen, it sounded like this. O-manna-manna-moon! O-manna-manna-moon!"

Annie started to laugh.

Suddenly there was a loud thump in the far corner of the room.

"Don't do that!" said a voice. "You mustn't!"

Stephen and Annie gasped. For there in the corner was a strange-looking creature, neither human nor animal, but small, rather hunched over, with long, dangly arms. They had not noticed it before because of the deep shadow in the corner of the room.

"What are you?" said Stephen.

"I'm the Oggamagog," said the creature. "I know you won't have heard of me before. I shouldn't be here at all. It's all a terrible mistake."

"Was that you making that funny noise last night?" said Stephen.

"I was chanting, if that is what you mean," said the Oggamagog. "That's how I keep myself company."

At that moment somebody started calling Stephen and Annie from upstairs.

"We'll have to go," said Annie. "But we'll come back later. Don't go away!" The children ran upstairs.

After breakfast they went back down into the basement. The Oggamagog had gone to sleep. But after a few minutes he woke up and said, "I'll tell you what an Oggamagog is. Oggamagogs are very, very old, and don't belong in this world. In the old days they were called upon by humans to answer their most difficult questions. Kings, princesses and knights used to come to us for advice. They could make us appear by turning anti-clockwise five times and chanting, 'O-manna-manna-moon!'

Even the common people used to call on us sometimes," said the Oggamagog, "when they wanted to know when to sow the crops or buy a pig. But I was a very ambitious Oggamagog. I told everyone I only wanted to be summoned for the most important questions and to be very well paid for it too. Oggamagogs aren't supposed to be paid, you see. It's against the rules.

One day the Great Oggamagog disguised himself as a poor man and called me to him. He asked me some silly questions about a cow that he'd seen at the market. I got very cross with him and said he was wasting my valuable time, and that he now owed me a thousand pounds. When he heard this the Great Oggamagog tore off his disguise and said: 'You have become far too big for your boots! Off with you! I am going to punish you by making you stay on earth with the humans. And for as long as I feel like it!' So here I am," said the Oggamagog. "I've lost count of the time, but oh dear, what a long time it has been."

"We are sorry," said Stephen.

"Is it really that bad, living with humans?" asked Annie. But before the Oggamagog could answer the children were called away again.

Later that morning Stephen said to Annie, "I wish there were some really important questions we could ask the Oggamagog. I want to test his powers. What can we ask?"

Annie thought for a while. "I don't know," she said.

That evening during dinner Stephen, who had been unusually quiet, suddenly said to his father, "Dad, is there anything very important that you need help or advice about?"

"What do you mean, Stephen?" said his father.

"Well, Annie and I have got to know a . . . er, someone who's terribly good at solving problems. But they have to be terribly difficult ones, not silly ones like . . ."

" . . . like deciding which tie you should wear tomorrow," said Annie.

Mr Bond laughed. "I see," he said thoughtfully. "Well, there is one problem I have right at the moment. I'm trying to decide which kind of lawnmower to buy to cut our great big new lawn."

"Oh, Dad," groaned Stephen. "Not that sort of thing."

"Sorry," said Mr Bond. "I can't help you then."

After supper Stephen and Annie went into Annie's room.

"The trouble is, Stephen," said Annie, "we just aren't important enough to think up a good question."

"I know what you mean," said Stephen. "There aren't any kings or knights anymore. There's no-one who can ask the Oggamagog a good question."

"Well, there is the Queen," said Annie.

"The Queen!" said Stephen, and he burst out laughing. "You mean get the Queen to talk to the Oggamagog?"

"I don't see why not," said Annie. "I bet she's tired of always talking to the same old people in the palace."

"You could be right," said Stephen. "I've got a postcard in my room. It's one I was supposed to send to Uncle Edward when we were on holiday in Cornwall, but I never did. Shall we send it to the Queen?"

"Oh yes!" shouted Annie, who was suddenly very excited. So they found the postcard and on it they wrote:

Your Majesty,
There is somebody very special living in the basement of our new house. He is called the Oggamagog. He is being punished by the Great Oggamagog. We think if you could only ask the Oggamagog a very difficult question and not give him any money for answering it he would be allowed to go home. Please write soon. Stephen and Annie Bond.

They posted the card the next day. Time passed and nothing happened. The children began to think they had been very silly to write to the Queen, who was probably having a good laugh over the card with her palace staff.

Then one day when they arrived home from school, they found their mother giving them a funny look when she opened the door. "There's something on the table for you two," she said.

Propped against the honey pot was a very white envelope, with a golden crown in the top left hand corner.

"We'll take it upstairs if you don't mind, Mum," said Annie. They were afraid their mother might want to know all about the Oggamagog if she saw the letter.

"Open it! Open it!" said Annie when they got to Stephen's room. Stephen opened the envelope very, very carefully. He wanted to keep it to show his new friends at school.

There was a small piece of white paper inside, folded very neatly. There was a short letter written on it, with a very large signature at the bottom with lots of squiggles.

"What does it say?" whispered Annie in awe.

Stephen read the letter aloud;

> "Dear Stephen and Annie,
> I don't think you need to worry about the Oggamagog any more. I have had a word with a very important person and he has assured me that the Oggamagog will be going home very soon. But just for fun, because I am sure you would like the Oggamagog to demonstrate his powers before he goes, why don't you ask him this, 'What must a Queen do to make all her subjects happy?'"

The children stared at the letter. The Queen had actually written to them!

"Come on!" shouted Stephen. "Let's go and show this to the Oggamagog!"

They went rushing headlong down into the basement, but the place where the Oggamagog had been on each of their visits was deserted.

"Look Stephen!" shouted Annie. "There's a piece of paper stuck on the windowsill!"

They ran over to look at it. Slowly Annie read out;

> "Dear Stephen and Annie,
> I only have time to scribble a quick note to wish you all the best. When the Great Oggamagog commands, one must obey at once. But if you do write back to Her Majesty, please tell her from me that the answer is; 'Nothing. Kings and Queens only make all their subjects happy in fairy stories.' Best wishes, The Oggamagog."

"You do realize, don't you Annie," said Stephen, "that the Oggamagog answered the Queen before we had shown him her letter?"

"Of course I do, stupid," said Annie.

"That's proof enough for me," said Stephen. "He was a very special person."

"Not a person," said Annie. "An Oggamagog."

There was silence for a few minutes.

"I wish he hadn't gone quite so soon," said Stephen. "I was going to ask him about Dad's lawnmower."

The Smelly Sock

Once there were three cousins who lived in the beautiful land of Italy. Their names were Rosa, Rita and Lola. Rosa and Rita were very rich, but Lola's father was only a fisherman, so her family were rather poor.

Shortly before Christmas, the girls' grandmother invited all three of them to spend the holidays with her in an old cottage in the hills.

Each of the girls was to bring with her some stuffing for the Christmas goose and a stocking to hang by the chimney.

Now in Italy, the children are not visited by Father Christmas. Instead their presents are brought to them by his dear old friend, the Befana.

The Befana is an ugly woman. Her nose is pointed like a witch's. There are warts on her face and wrinkles on her cheek. But she's very kind. Every Christmas she fills her shopping bag with presents and flies with them over the rooftops. When she comes to a house, the Befana puts her nose to the chimney. And, if she smells a good smell – like roasting chestnuts or toasting muffins – she tiptoes into the house and fills the children's stockings with gifts.

"I hear the Befana has lots of nice gifts to give this year," Grandma said as she showed the children to their room and helped them hang up their stockings by the fireplace.

"I'm sure she'll leave me the best presents when she sees my stocking," boasted Rosa. "I spent all my pocket money on it. It's made from pure silk and there's a diamond sewn into it because it once belonged to a princess. The Befana would be flattered to fill such a stocking."

"You might have spent your pocket money on a costly stocking," argued Rita, "but I spent mine on a yarn of expensive wool that stretches like elastic. I shall surely get more presents than you."

"I'm afraid I've only brought one of my brother's socks," said Lola, who had never received a gift in all her life and so would have been pleased with anything. "It's a bit smelly and there's a hole in the toe, so I can't expect much."

"I'm sure the Befana will give you what she thinks you deserve," Grandma assured the girls. "Now come and have some supper, all of you."

The children left the room and closed the door behind them. While they were eating, the Befana came down the chimney and looked closely at the stockings.

"This one must belong to a princess," she said, feeling the diamond in Rosa's stocking. "Surely a rich princess needs no gifts except maybe a few bones for her dog."

And she filled Rosa's stocking with old bones.

Then she saw Rita's extra large stocking. "This must belong to an old woman like me," the Befana said. "What would an old lady want for Christmas except, maybe, a few toothache pills and an extra pair of dentures?"

And she filled the large stocking with old teeth and a packet of large pills that tasted horribly like bitter almonds.

At last the Befana saw Lola's smelly sock. "Ah," she cried. "Now here is someone who needs all the help they can get." And she darned the old sock with silver thread and filled it up to the brim with toys and sweets, and lots of little golden wishing stars that can make your every wish come true.

Little Lola is still wishing upon those enchanted stars to this very day.

The Candle

Tilly's father Josef, was the King's candlemaker. Whenever King Magnus had important guests, he asked Josef to make a special candle for the dinner table, and soon it was known far and wide that King Magnus had the best candlemaker in the world.

One day Josef was summoned to the palace. When he arrived the Chamberlain rushed him in to see the King snapping, "Don't dawdle!" It was clear that King Magnus was in a very bad mood.

"The candlemaker, Your Majesty," said the Chamberlain, bowing almost to the floor as he backed out of the room as fast as he could.

"Hah!" said King Magnus.

"Hah, Your Majesty?" said Josef. He was not a man to be frightened by bad-tempered Kings.

"I thought you were supposed to be the best candlemaker in the world," scoffed the King.

"Others have been kind enough to say so," replied Josef.

"Well, they were wrong," said King Magnus as he stamped his foot angrily. "I've just had dinner with King Adolphus of Lemburg, and he had a candle on his dinner table so big that the table sagged in the middle."

"That must have made eating your dinner very uncomfortable, Your Majesty," said Josef mildly.

"Well, it did. But that's not the point," King Magnus thumped the arm of his throne. "The point is – he challenged me to a candle-making contest. When I say me, I mean you, of course."

"Naturally, Your Majesty," replied Josef.

"You have to come up with the tallest candle in the world by tomorrow. Now, off you go. Get on with it!"

Josef went home and started work while Tilly went into the forest to gather sticks for his fire.

Deep in the forest she came upon an old woman sitting at the foot of a tree. Beside her lay a hand cart with a broken wheel.

"Can I help you?" asked Tilly.

"Like you I've been gathering sticks," said the old woman. "But the wheel struck a large stone, and the wood is split."

"I'll drag it back to our cottage," said Tilly. "My father will mend it for you."

When Tilly arrived home, Josef was hard at work making the King's candle.

"Father, I met this poor old woman in the forest, and her hand cart is broken," said Tilly. "Will you mend it for her?"

Josef looked at the broken wheel. He thought of all the candle-making he had to do before tomorrow.

"Of course I will," he said and by midnight the hand cart was as good as new.

"It's too late for you to go home now," said Tilly. "Stay with us until morning."

"I cannot," said the old woman. "I can see how busy your father is."

"Please stay," said Josef. "I shall be working late to make the tallest candle in the world for King Magnus, but I won't disturb you."

"You are very kind," said the old woman. "May you have magic in your fingers tonight."

The old woman slept in Tilly's box bed. Tilly lay on the rug beside the fire while Josef worked on until dawn.

When Tilly awoke the next morning, she blinked in amazement.

"Oh, Father!" she exclaimed. "What a beautiful candle!"

The candle stood taller than Tilly and Josef had decorated it with scenes from the forest. Bears and wolves lurked behind trees. Birds perched on long, curved branches. Rabbits and squirrels peeped out among the flowers and mosses growing on the forest floor.

Then the old woman woke up and came to look.

"It is very good," she said, smiling. "Now, I must go home."

Josef and Tilly walked a little way into the forest with her, and the sun was high in the sky before they returned.

As they drew near to their cottage, they heard scuffling. Two boys ran out of the back door and away down the path. Josef pushed open the cottage door and gave a cry of dismay when he saw what had happened.

The candle was alight and was dripping onto the floor.

"What will King Magnus say?" groaned Josef. "My work is ruined."

"No, Father!" cried Tilly and she tugged at his arms excitedly. "Look at the animals. They're moving!"

And so they were. The bears and wolves prowled about between the trees. The birds flew from branch to branch singing. Rabbits and squirrels scampered around, and from every flower the droning of bees could be heard. Josef blew out the candle and the forest scene was still.

"Do you remember what the old woman said?" asked Tilly. "May you have magic in your fingers! And you have! Now we must hurry to the palace."

In the great Hall, King Adolphus' candle already blazed with light. It was a copy of his castle at Lemburg. Every turret had its own wick so the candle was covered in tiny points of flame.

"Is that it?" snapped King Magnus when he saw Josef's candle. "Well, I suppose it's quite pretty."

"Thank you," said Josef.

"But it's not very big, is it?" went on King Magnus.

Josef carried his candle up to the other end of the Great Hall, and lit it.

"And it's only got one wick," complained King Magnus.

Once again the scenes of the forest came to life before their astonished eyes.

King Adolphus made a very handsome speech, saying of course, King Magnus had won the contest. He hoped King Magnus realised what a great candle-maker Josef was, and if he ever forgot, Josef would always be welcome at the palace of Lemburg.

King Magnus suddenly thought he would have to be better-tempered in future. He gave Josef four hundred gold crowns, and said Tilly could come to the palace whenever she wanted to play with Princess Clara.

Bran Bear in the Snow

It was winter. Bran bear lay snuggled between his father and mother. But he was wide awake, and bored.

"I'm going to see what it is like outside," he finally decided.

Quietly, he crawled out from between his sleeping parents. He then padded towards the mouth of the cave. As he peered out he caught his breath. He blinked. He rubbed his eyes. No, he wasn't dreaming; the whole world was white!

Bran had never seen snow before.

"Wow, it's beautiful!" he gasped, in awe. It was as if he were looking at a giant Christmas card.

Trembling with excitement, he cautiously rolled down the gentle slope just below the cave entrance.

"Brrr!" he shivered, realizing how cold the snow was.

But he liked the soft feel of this strange, powdery stuff. Playfully, he began to paw at the snow. He then dug his whole head in it. Ptchooo! it made him sneeze. And when he tried to bite it, it immediately melted in his mouth. It tasted just like cold water, he thought, licking his jaws.

After playing in the snow for a while, Bran decided to explore the nearby wood. He had never been there before and he might find a companion to play with. So off he loped. It was hard to run in the snow, he found out, reaching the edge of the wood exhausted.

66

Panting hard, Bran paused for a rest. He peered into the wood, ears pricked, listening. All was quiet.

"You'll find no one in there," said a voice above him. "Go home, young bear!"

Startled, Bran looked up. He saw a crow perched on a snow-laden branch of a pine tree. She was looking down at him with scolding eyes.

"Go home!" she croaked again, more sharply. "Go home, young bear, before some harm comes to you!" And so saying, she flew off, the flapping of her wings echoing loudly in the silence.

Bran merely shrugged. And, ignoring the crow's advice, he entered the wood. "I'm not scared," he told himself as he plodded through the snow.

Deeper and deeper into the wood he ventured. But he saw no one. And he heard no one. The wood was totally deserted.

A light wind rose. As it blew through the trees it made eerie sounds, like wailing ghosts. Bran didn't like that. Now and then he started when snow fell off tree branches and plopped to the ground. He began to feel scared – all alone in a deserted wood.

Just then, however, he heard voices. He paused to listen, to make sure. Yes, he could hear voices. Distant voices which rose and fell with the wind. Joyfully, Bran set off running. He did not stop until he reached the edge of the wood.

Peering from behind a bank of snow, he saw children playing not far away. He could hear their excited cries. They seemed to be having fun, he thought. So he joined them.

Some children were skating on a frozen pond. Curious, Bran stood to watch. He then decided to have a go himself.

Carefully, he stepped on to the ice. It was stone hard, he found out. And slippery. Bump! He fell on his bottom. He tried to get up again, only to fall once more.

The children laughed, amused.

Bran struggled for quite a while before he finally managed to stay up on his feet. He then tried to skate. But it wasn't that easy as he soon found out. He skated on his bottom . . . He skated on his back . . . He skated on his tummy. But never on his feet.

All the time the children laughed.

Finally Bran gave up. Hurting all over, he clambered off the pond. He then waddled further away to where a group of children were having a snowball fight. He thought it was very funny. Every time a snowball hit a boy or a girl he clapped.

"Why not join in?" he decided after watching for a while.

Making a snowball wasn't as easy as he had thought. Not with plump paws. But in the end he managed to make one. After choosing a big boy as a target, he threw the snowball with all his might. He missed.

The big boy, however, saw what Bran had intended to do. He already had a huge snowball in one hand. He was a good shot, too. WHAM! The snowball hit Bran full in the face. He tumbled backwards, more surprised than hurt.

Hardly able to see, he scrambled to his feet, ready to fight back. But by now every boy and girl had seen him, and he became their only target. Poor Bran found himself being hit all over. He had no choice but to run away.

Presently he came across more children, bob-sleighing down a steep slope. Fascinated, he stood up to watch. 'I'd love to have a go!' he thought.

Just then he spotted a free sledge at the top of the slope. Without a moment's hesitation, he ran towards it, clambered inside and – zoom! down he went.

"Hey, that's my sledge!" someone shouted. But Bran was already half way down the slope, travelling at a high speed. He could hardly breathe and the fur on his head stood on end. He thought it was a marvellous feeling.

Bran's sledge did not stop at the bottom of the slope as most others did. It went careering along the snow, still at a high speed. On and on it skidded . . . until it finally bumped into a huge snowman that some children had just finished building. It collapsed altogether, burying most of Bran.

"You stupid bear!" scolded the children, furiously. "You've ruined our snowman!"

Bran knew he had done something naughty. Scrambling to his feet, he fled as fast as his stumpy legs could carry him. He did not stop running until he reached the safety of the wood.

Luckily, he found his old footprints. Following them, he started his journey back home. He was feeling quite miserable now; cold, bedraggled and aching all over.

To add to his misery it began to snow; lightly at first, then more and more heavily. The wind grew stronger too, until it became a howling fury. Soon Bran found himself in the midst of a blizzard. Treacherous snowdrifts lay about, and he fell into one of them. Only his head showed as he desperately strove to get out. But all in vain.

Numb with cold and totally exhausted, he remained helplessly stuck in the snowdrift. How he wished he had listened to the crow's advice. He wished he had never left home in the first place. None of this would've happened. He hated the snow now.

He was barely conscious when two huge, furry paws carefully picked him out of the snow. He opened his eyes, ever so slowly.

"I-is that . . . you, Daddy?" he asked in a weak, trembling voice.

"Yes, it's me," replied Father Bear.

"Oh, I'm so glad." Bran buried his face in his father's chest and began to cry.

"Hush, son, hush," said Father Bear soothingly. "You are alright now."

"I want to go home," sobbed Bran. "I want to go home and never, ever go out in the snow again. Please, Daddy, take me home."

"We are going home, son," said Father Bear. "We are going home."

The Proud Little Pig

A Piggy one day,
In the fair month of May,
Won a prize at an animal show.
Round her neck the judge tied,
A blue ribbon wide,
With a beautiful blue satin bow.

Back home to the sty,
Piggy went by and by,
To be with the other pigs there.
"They are just common pork,"
Piggy said with a snort.
"They can't expect me to stay here."

That Piggy so proud,
Her head in a cloud,
Grunted and sniffed with disdain.
With a gleam in her eye,
She walked out of the sty,
Vowing never to live there again.

Now a Wolf lived nearby,
And this Pig he did spy,
Trotting so proud down the lane.
He drooled at the thought,
Of lovely roast pork,
As he eyed that poor piggy so vain.

The Wolf he was sly,
And as Piggy went by,
He bowed to her, low from the waist.
"Dear Piggy," said he,
"Pray won't you tell me
Where you're off to in such a great haste?"

72

"To the city," said she.
"So that people may see
What a marvellous Piggy I am!"
With slavering jaws,
The Wolf rubbed his paws,
While his cunning mind thought of a plan.

"Dear Piggy, I think,"
Said the Wolf with a wink,
"That you should be Queen of the land.
You should wear a fine gown,
Splendid jewels and a crown,
And live as befits one so grand."

"Sweet Piggy," said he,
"If you come home with me,
You shall be Queen of my castle."
"Lead the way," said the Pig,
And go with him she did,
That cunning old Wolf was a rascal.

Now that proud little Pig,
Danced a very fine jig,
While the Wolf played a tune on his flute.
With a curtsy, a twirl,
Piggy waltzed, Piggy whirled,
As the Wolf tootled, toot-te-toot-toot.

On danced the Pig,
With a jiggerty-jig,
Poor vain little blue ribbon winner.
When near to his den, the Wolf pounced
And then . . .
Sat down to roast pork for his dinner.

A Cold Christmas

It was Christmas Eve and Gelda, who lived deep in the Scottish countryside, was very sad. She was sad because the weather was mild and sunny when her friend Hassan, who had come for Christmas, had been looking forward to a cold, snowy Christmas. Hassan lived in a hot country and had hot Christmases.

"Where is the snow?" he asked sadly, remembering the winter scenes on the Christmas cards that Gelda sent him every year. On the plane he had looked forward to crunching through deep snow, with pheasants and robins everywhere. He even imagined himself riding on a sleigh through the snow.

"I wish it would freeze," sighed Gelda. "What can we do?"

"Well you can't write to Jack Frost as you do to Father Christmas," said Gelda's mother.

"Yes we can!" cried Gelda. "And we will!" So the two children sat down and wrote to Jack Frost. They slipped the letter into the coldest place they could think of in the house – the freezer.

Jack Frost knew nothing of the letter. He peeped through the window of his icy cavern deep in the side of the mountain. He was very lazy and only went out when he had to.

"I'm divinely cold and comfortable," he said, as he slid onto his icy bed and sucked an ice lolly. He had an icicle on the end of his nose and icicles at the tips of his fingers and toes. His feet were on a stone cold water bottle. He was reading 'The Horrors of a Hot Climate'.

The freezer, however, did find the letter and it sent out one of the little freezer frosties to take it to Jack Frost. It was a dangerous journey. The sun might melt the frostie as it went on its secret way. It eventually arrived safely and handed the letter to Jack Frost. Jack read it:

DEAR JACK FROST, PLEASE SEND US A COLD CHRISTMAS. LOVE FROM GELDA AND HASSAN.

Jack Frost thanked the little frostie, refroze it and sent it back to the freezer. 'Somebody sending me love,' thought Jack Frost. The thought of it nearly melted the icicle on the end of his nose.

He opened up his iced window. Rooks called from the remains of last year's nests. He must wait for the white moon to turn to gold. Then he put on his ice coat and filled his pockets with ice cubes. He took his frost spray, his paint brush, his skates and other icy items and cold foot, off he went.

He froze the ground as he walked. He flung ice cubes into the streams. He rushed about, spraying wildly in all directions. Everything sparkled in the cold moonlight. He flung freezing air at sleeping geese, hens and goats. He sprayed huddled sheep. They looked over their cold shoulders in surprise.

He froze a flooded field. Then saying to himself, "All work and no play makes Jack a dull boy," he put on his skates.

He skated furiously fast, leaning forward like a champion skater until the icicle on his nose nearly met the icicles on his toes. 'No one can skate like Jack Frost,' he thought.

Then he got on with his work. "This will be the coldest Christmas Scotland has ever known," he decided. At the windows of the scattered houses he flipped his paint brush, flicking frozen ferns and feathers onto the glass. 'I'm a wonderful artist,' he thought, considering his handywork.

Suddenly he heard voices. "This is the coldest carol singing I've ever known," complained one singer.

"No one warned us about the sudden change in the weather," said the other. Their breath was like white feathers.

Jack Frost did not often meet humans. He decided to make friends with them. He shook them by the hand. "Ouch! my hand is tingling with cold," cried one.

"My nose feels as if someone has rubbed it with ice," groaned the other.

Jack stood on their feet. "My feet have gone numb!" They jumped up and down, throwing Jack Frost off so that he slithered away on his ice coat over the frozen ground. He was disappointed. He left them with a sound like a 'whoosh'. Icefoot he went, over the fields, thinking of Siberia and icebergs and the South Pole. He sucked a glacier mint. He was very pleased with his work.

He went home and had a nice, ice cold bath. Then he lay on his slippery bed and enjoyed the frozen fish finger the little frostie had brought him.
He thought about the love the children had sent him. A tear came from his eye and immediately froze. It clattered down his cheek and fell with a tinkling

sound onto the floor.

"I must be careful," he said, "or this love will melt my heart. Then there will be no more Jack Frost, no more cold Christmases. After all, the children must have a cold Christmas."

On Christmas morning when the shutters were opened, Hassan and Gelda shouted with joy. They warmed a coin and made a spy hole on the frosted window. They peeped through at the frozen world outside.

"Just what we wanted for Christmas," they shouted happily. They wrapped themselves up and went out. They came to the frozen field. "Look! Let's slide."

They ran and fell about on the ice. They saw the marks made by Jack Frost's skates. They said, "Someone has been skating in the night. That's strange!"

When they got home Gelda's mother said, "Well, Jack Frost has certainly answered your letter."

They ran to the freezer. The letter had gone.

"Thank you, Jack Frost," cried Gelda and Hassan. Then they ran out laughing, into the cold Christmas garden to play.

Father Christmas' Dilemma

In a far and distant land, covered in ice and snow, there is a very high mountain which glistens in the sunlight and sparkles in the moonlight. On the highest peak, in a castle made of ice, lives King Frost.

Lower down on the side of the mountain, in a pine forest, there is a small house and a stable. It is the home of Father Christmas and his two reindeer, Robert and Rufus.

Inside, Father Christmas was very busy, preparing all the toys for the children, and Uncle Holly and Auntie Ivy had come up from the village to help him. Suddenly there was a very loud rat-tat-tat on the door.

"That must be Malcolm the milkman," exclaimed Auntie Ivy. "But he sounds very impatient this morning." As she opened the door she could see poor Malcolm dripping from head to foot. "Whatever is the matter?" she asked in amazement. "You look as if you have fallen into a stream."

"The snow is melting," wept Malcolm. "Along the forest path, I sank in right up to my waist. I can't deliver any more milk today," he added as a puddle formed at his feet.

Auntie Ivy invited the very wet milkman in to dry himself by the roaring log fire. "I'm just going to make some hot chocolate, so you must join us," she told him.

As they sat around the fire enjoying Auntie Ivy's home-made nut cookies and sipping their hot drinks, Father Christmas suddenly looked very worried.

"If the snow is melting, I won't be able to get my sleigh out, as it will sink," he said in a very doleful voice.

"Oh dear," sighed Auntie Ivy. "Tomorrow night the children will be hanging up their stockings and it would be terrible if they woke up on Christmas morning to find them empty."

Uncle Holly looked up from the corner of the fireplace where he was sitting listening to the discussion and exclaimed, "We must get in touch with King Frost. He is in charge of the weather in the Ice Kingdom."

"But how can we reach King Frost?" asked Father Christmas. "I can't use my sleigh and it would take me too long to walk. Christmas Day would be over before I could get there."

At that moment there was a sharp knock on the door. It was Percy Pigeon tapping with his beak. He had come to deliver some more air mail letters from the children for Father Christmas. "Come in," said Auntie Ivy, "and have some cookies and hot chocolate before you fly off on your way."

Suddenly Father Christmas, Uncle Holly and Auntie Ivy looked at each other and smiled. An idea had struck them all at the same time.

79

"Percy," said Father Christmas, "I wonder if you could do us a great service and fly up to King Frost with an urgent message?" Father Christmas then told Percy of his dilemma.

The pigeon said he would go at once and, whilst he was pecking up the last of the nut cookies, Father Christmas wrote a note to King Frost saying,

"SNOW-WAY MELTING. WILL BE UNABLE TO USE SLEIGH AND REINDEER FOR TOY DELIVERY ON CHRISTMAS EVE. PLEASE HELP! FATHER CHRISTMAS."

After they had waved goodbye to Percy and wished him a speedy flight, Father Christmas sat down by the fire to read the letters the pigeon postman had delivered.

"Goodness me!" he exclaimed after a few minutes. "Baseball bats are very popular this year. I must go into the workshop straight away and make a dozen more. Would you like to help me, Malcolm?" he asked the milkman who was now quite dry again.

Before Malcolm had time to reply, Father Christmas called Auntie Ivy and asked her to fetch some more dolls, teddy bears and skipping ropes from the store and Uncle Holly was sent to collect a further supply of footballs, trains and motor cars.

Whilst all this activity was going on below, Percy was flying higher and higher to the top of the mountain. His wings were aching by the time he reached the ice castle and he had only just about enough strength left to knock on the door with his beak.

After waiting several minutes Percy heard a very loud yawn which rocked the walls of the castle. Then the big door opened slowly and King Frost stood there with his crown of icicles dripping down his face.

"Oh dear," he said, stifling another yawn. "I've overslept, and everything is melting around me," he added as he looked at the pool of water at his feet.

Percy told him that he had an urgent message from Father Christmas and the King invited him into the castle whilst he read it.

"Oh dear," he said again. "It is all my fault. We were having a birthday party for the Queen last night and we were all so tired that we didn't hear our alarm clocks this morning. I must call the Ice Council at once."

King Frost then flung open the window and in the loudest and most bellowing voice that Percy had ever heard, summoned the North Wind and the ice fairies to the castle.

Almost immediately there was a cold gust of air and a flurry of snow and ice as the wind blew in amidst thousands of silvery wings.

In a very frosty voice the King told them that Father Christmas desperately needed their help and ordered them to return to work straight away.

"Now, Percy," said the King. "You must join the Queen and I for a supper-time breakfast. Then you must have a good night's rest before starting your flight back."

Meanwhile, down in the forest, Father Christmas was feeding Robert and Rufus before going to bed. "I do believe I can feel the North Wind getting up," he declared. "That surely means that snow is on the way." He hurried back into the house to tell the good news to Uncle Holly and Auntie Ivy.

The next morning when they all got up, they discovered that Father Christmas had been right. The forest was covered in a thick blanket of snow.

"How wonderful," said Father Christmas. "Percy must have delivered my message to King Frost. We can start loading the sleigh straight away."

They worked hard all day, sorting out the toys and packing them on to the sleigh. By nightfall their task was complete.

The moon was shining brightly in the sky as Father Christmas with Robert and Rufus, prepared to leave on his long journey. But just as Uncle Holly and Auntie Ivy got to the door to wave him goodbye, there was a flutter of wings and Percy pigeon landed at their feet.

"We are so grateful to you, Percy," beamed Father Christmas. "It is thanks to you that the children's stockings will be filled in time for Christmas morning," he called out as the reindeer started to gallop off. "And don't forget to hang up your stocking, Percy. I am putting a special present in it . . . A big box of Auntie Ivy's home-made nut cookies!"

The Boxing Day Hunt

One chilly morning in mid-winter, Max McBrush was still asleep when Jacko the crow flew overhead and dropped something into his warm den. Max woke with a start. He looked around and saw a small stone with a piece of paper wrapped round it. He quickly untied the string and unfolded the piece of paper.

"So Humphrey wants to come and visit me," said Max. "I thought that brother of mine would be much too high and mighty to visit after living so long in the city. But I'm glad he's coming, anyway," he added.

Then an awful thought crossed Max's mind. Humphrey was coming for Christmas. That meant he would be with him on Boxing Day, the day dreaded by every fox in the neighbourhood. For it was on Boxing Day that the hunt took place. But it was too late to stop Humphrey, who was arriving the next day.

Max went in search of his friends – Charlie Badger, Ettie Hedgehog, Nicholas Weasel and Miranda Owl – to tell them about his brother's visit.

"How are we going to make sure Humphrey doesn't get into trouble on Boxing Day?" asked Max.

After a few minutes Miranda Owl said, "The best thing would be for your brother to hide in the hayloft at the Robertsons' farm. They needn't know anything about it, and as long as Humphrey doesn't leave his scent on the way to the farm, all should be well."

"Good thinking," said Max. He suddenly felt much happier.

84

The next day Max went up to the road to meet Humphrey. Soon he heard the rattling of wheels and round a bend in the road came a pony trap. In the back stood Humphrey, and behind him Max could make out several bulky objects. As the trap came closer Max saw with dismay that they were large suitcases.

"Max!" boomed Humphrey. "How marvellous to see you again."

"You look awfully overdressed for the country," said Max. "and all that luggage."

"Well, I can never decide what to bring," replied Humphrey. "So I have to bring everything."

"We've got a bit of a problem," said Max as they went down towards his den, struggling with the suitcases. "There's going to be a big hunt here on Boxing Day."

"But Max," exclaimed Humphrey. "I love watching hunts. All those red coats and shining horses. All those silly hounds with their tongues hanging out."

"Don't be ridiculous Humphrey," said Max crossly. "You can't watch the hunt. You're a fox for heaven's sake!"

"Yes, but if I dress up in all my finery they're not going to know I'm a fox, are they?" said Humphrey.

"I wish you'd behave like a real fox," said Humphrey.

"Oh Max, what a spoilsport you are." Humphrey sighed dramatically. "Let's just enjoy Christmas Day, and then we'll decide what to do."

Christmas Day was a happy day for the two brothers, for they were fond of each other, inspite of their differences. But then Boxing Day arrived.

"Wake up, Humphrey!" said Max. "We've got to go up to the Robertsons' farm."

"Why?" said Humphrey. "Are we going to collect eggs?"

"Yes," said Max, which was a lie, but he had to get Humphrey to safety.

"I want you to come and see something in the hayloft," said Max. Humphrey went along obediently, thinking there must be something very interesting there.

"Now listen," said Max when they were in the hayloft. "I want you to hide yourself in that big pile of hay over there until the hunt is over."

"Oh, Max!" burst out Humphrey.

"Please Humphrey, do as I say," pleaded Max, and then he ran back to his den before Humphrey could argue with him any more.

Humphrey stayed in the hayloft for all of five minutes, then came out, brushing the hay from his fine clothes.

86   "Now to find the hunt!" he said.

He climbed up to the top of a small hill, where there was a large oak tree. From there he had a splendid view of the surrounding countryside. He was wearing his favourite pale blue jacket and trousers and a red scarf. He stood out for miles. Soon Humphrey heard the huntsman's horn.

When the hunt came into sight Humphrey decided to wave to the huntsmen and hounds. For the truth was that Humphrey really did forget he was a fox sometimes.

At the sight of Humphrey on the hill the hounds pulled up sharply.

"What's that?" asked one hound.

"Looks like a fox, all dressed up," said another, and at once they all set off up the hill in hot pursuit.

"Dash it!" said Humphrey. "I'd better climb the tree."

Soon the whole pack of hounds was below him baying furiously.

"Can't you see, you stupid hounds," yelled Humphrey, "that I'm not a fox at all!"

"Well, you look like a fox!" barked one hound.

"And you smell like a fox!" yelped another.

"Smell like a fox?" said Humphrey. "Oh no I don't." And he took from his back pocket a bottle of perfume and sprinkled it over the hounds.

"No fox ever smelled like that," shouted the lead hound. "Let's go!"

As soon as the hounds had vanished from sight Humphrey climbed down the tree. Then he sauntered over to Max's den.

"Max!" he bellowed. "Max!" But there was silence. The den was empty.

Suddenly Humphrey heard the sound of panting. Turning round he was surprised to see Nicholas Weasel standing there, all out of breath.

"They're after Max!" gasped Nicholas. "When Max saw the hounds were after you he came out of his den to distract them. He saved your life, and now he is in danger!"

"What a chump!" said Humphrey. "Still, that was rather nice of him, though I think in fact I saved my own life with my bottle of perfume."

"Your brother is running for his life at this very moment," said Nicholas Weasel.

"No he isn't," said Humphrey. "He's right here." Indeed, along the hedgerow came a very wet, bedraggled Max.

"What a mess you're in!" shouted Humphrey. "What happened?"

"I had to hide from the hounds by diving into the pond and holding my breath long enough for them to give up," spluttered Max. "I thought my lungs were going to burst."

"What a splendid trick!" said Humphrey. "It's almost as good as mine."

"And what was your trick, Humphrey?" asked Max. So Humphrey told him about the bottle of perfume and how it had tricked the hounds, and Max started to laugh, and soon all three of them were laughing until the tears fell down their cheeks.

"You know what, Max?" said Humphrey. "Next year I'm going to bring my motorbike and give those hounds a real run for their money."

"Next year?" gasped Max. "You mean you're coming back?"

"Of course," replied Humphrey, beaming. "I've never had so much fun in all my life!"

Max shook his head. He really did wonder sometimes if living in the city hadn't completely scrambled his brother's brains.

Fred Throws a Party

FRED stood in the corner of the kitchen gurgling quietly. In the old days, Mum often said, she would have used a cooker to make their meals. Potatoes and carrots in saucepans of boiling water and meat roasting in the oven.

Chris laughed at the thought of such an old-fashioned way of doing things.

"What hard work it must have been," he said.

"I suppose it was," said Mum. "But lots of people enjoyed it."

"I'd rather have FRED," said Chris. "Food Requested and Electronically Delivered." He read the words on FRED's side. "All you have to do is press the right button."

"And you and Tod would have hamburgers every day, I know," said Mum.

Chris longed to operate FRED himself. He wanted to turn FRED's yellow arrow, press the red button and wait for the door in FRED's middle to slide open revealing hamburgers or, if Mum was choosing, beef stew and vegetables.

One day Mum had to go out suddenly. Grandma had had an accident and was in hospital.

"Will you get lunch today, Chris?" asked Mum. "Tod will be in soon. He's playing with his friends."

"Can I use FRED?" asked Chris at once.

"Of course," said Mum. "Now listen carefully. Turn the yellow arrow to the type of food you want, and then press the red button twice – once for you and once for Tod."

"Simple," said Chris. "Tell Grandma I hope she's soon feeling better."
Before long Tod came in.

"I'm hungry," he said. "What's for lunch?"

"Whatever you like," said Chris.

"Great. I'll have hamburger and chips and icecream cake," replied Tod.

"That sounds fine to me," said Chris. He turned FRED's yellow arrow to hamburger and chips and icecream cake. "Now, we want enough for two." Chris pressed the red button twice.

At that moment the videophone bleeped. Chris went into the hall to answer it. "Watch out for the food," he called to Tod.

It was Mum on the videophone calling from the hospital. "Grandma's feeling much better. I'll plug you in so you can talk to her."

Mum disappeared from the screen and Chris could see his granny sitting up in bed. Her right arm was bandaged up to the shoulder.

"Hello, Chris," said Granny. "Are you looking after your little brother?"

"Yes," replied Chris. "He's watching FRED for me." They talked for a few minutes, then Chris said goodbye and went back to the kitchen.

"Is lunch ready yet?" he asked.

"No," said Tod crossly. "And I'm starving."

Suddenly they heard a loud clunk. The door in FRED's middle slid open and two parcels of hamburgers and chips appeared.

"Hooray," shouted Tod. "At last!"

Then two more parcels appeared and two more and two more.

Hamburgers and chips began to cascade out of FRED. They rolled across the kitchen floor and piled up against the door.

"Switch FRED off," cried Tod.

"I don't know how," said Chris, just as a huge slab of icecream cake – enough for twenty people – oozed out of FRED's door, followed by another and another.

FRED gave a deep contented gurgle, churned on for a few more moments and then stopped.

"Quick Tod, help me to pick this food up," said Chris.

Soon the kitchen table was stacked high with the parcels of hamburgers and chips.

"Put the icecream cake in the freezer," said Chris. "I'm going to make a few video-calls."

Tod did as he was told while Chris called ten of his friends. They each passed the message on to four other friends.

Very soon the kitchen was full to bursting with boys and girls eating hamburgers and chips and icecream cake.

Mum could hardly believe her eyes when she walked into the kitchen.

"What a party!" she said. "How did you get all this food? Didn't you press the right buttons on FRED?"

"I'm sure I did," said Chris. "I ordered hamburger and chips and icecream cake, for two. But FRED sent enough for fifty."

"I can't understand it," said Mum, and she ordered one cup of coffee.

FRED's door opened.

Everyone stood back.

FRED delivered one cup of coffee.

"Well, it's a mystery," said Mum.

"I don't think it is," said a small voice. It was Tod.

"Whatever do you mean?" asked Chris.

"You see that red button," said Tod. "I didn't know that it was used to tell FRED how many people he had to feed."

"I see," said Mum, trying not to smile.

"And I pressed it lots and lots of times."

"About fifty?" asked Chris.

"Well, I thought it would make FRED hurry up. I was so hungry," wailed Tod.

Mum began to laugh. Chris and his friends joined in.

Tod cheered up at once. "It's been a lovely party, hasn't it?" he said.

And everyone laughed as Fred gurgled in the corner.

Bonnie and the Chico

Bonnie Aldridge lived on the Moon. She led a lonely life until she got her Chico, one of the special robots programmed to be a child's companion.

When it arrived, she liked it at once. Its head was dome-shaped with scanners instead of eyes, sensors instead of ears and it had a body containing computer units. It looked very lovable, almost cuddly. It was never bored, it never argued or sulked, it remembered things for Bonnie and helped her.

Every morning when the pillow alarm woke her, the Chico switched itself on. While Bonnie took her shower, the Chico got out her clothes and waited while she dressed. Then they went to the kitchen and Bonnie dialled her breakfast. After that she did her lessons at her computer terminal while the Chico clicked and whirred storing information. At homework time if Bonnie forgot anything, the Chico's memory banks supplied the answer. Bonnie worked hard. If she didn't do well, she knew she would have to go to boarding school on earth.

Every night, Bonnie's mother told her a story about space travel, alien adventures or engineering projects; or stories of old-time earth cowboys or pirates or fairy tales. For the fairy tales, she explained magic which children on the Moon in the 21st century couldn't understand. These were Bonnie's favourites, but when she wrote fairy tales for homework, she got low marks.

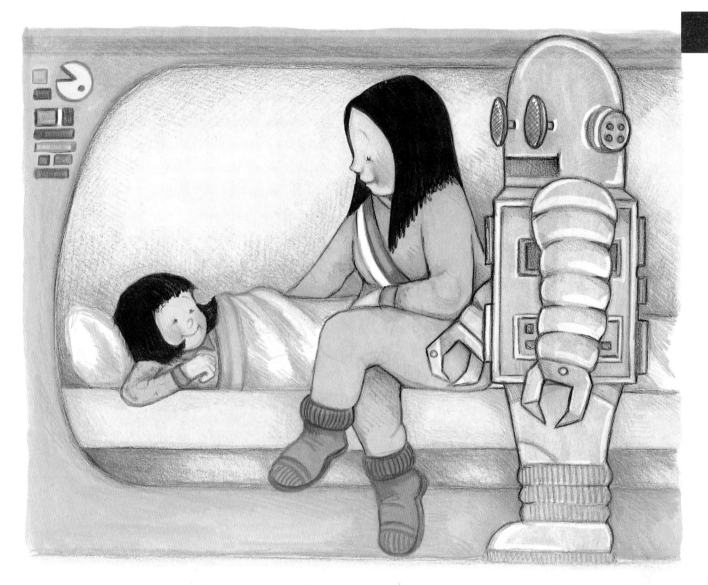

While Bonnie lay snug in bed, the robot listened too, and stored the stories in its memory banks but the first time it heard a fairy tale, it muttered metalically, "This does not compute."

After Mrs. Aldridge had gone, the Chico said, "That story did not compute, Bonnie. I do not have enough data."

Bonnie said sleepily, "What do you want to know, Chico?"

"What is a prince?"

"The son of a king, the head of the community."

Chico whirred and clicked. "What is a charger?"

"A horse, a creature that the prince rides."

Chirrr-clk. "What is a dragon?"

"A fire-breathing monster."

"And a dwarf?"

"A . . . small . . . magic . . . person . . ." But before she had finished, Bonnie was asleep.

Next morning the Chico asked questions until it understood fairy tales.

Time passed. Bonnie did her lessons with the Chico's help, played games and shared bed-time stories with it. She became so fond of it that she couldn't imagine life without it.

One day when Mrs. Aldridge was held up at work she called Bonnie on the vision-phone and told her to put herself to bed and run a video instead of having a story but Bonnie had a better idea. When she was in bed she said, "Chico, please tell me one of Mummy's stories."

The Chico whirred and clicked and began in his metallic voice, "Long, long ago, the son of the Moonbase Director . . ."

"That's not one of Mummy's stories."

"Yes, it is," said the Chico. "It's about a prince, the son of the most important man in the community. Don't interrupt, you will disrupt my circuits."

Bonnie realised that the Chico had changed the fairy tale words into terms he had been programmed to use. This sounded as if it would be fun, she promised not to interrupt.

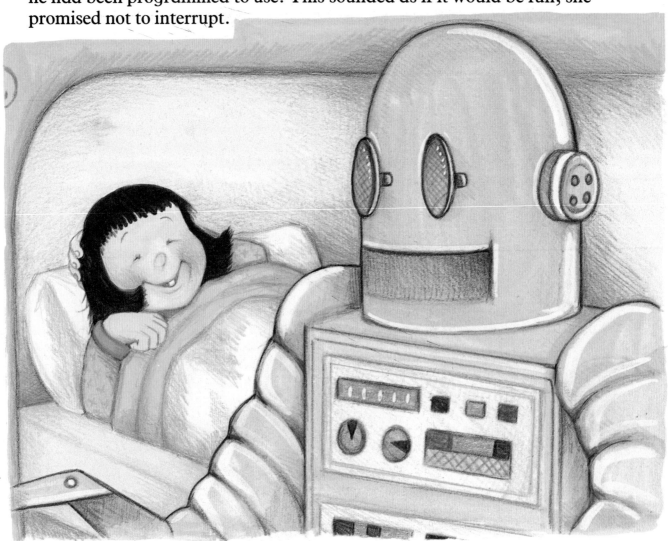

"Gid, the Moonbase Director's son decided it was time to make his way in the community so he set out in search of adventure. Climbing into his dashing white Moon-buggy he drove north. He had heard that the daughter of a Planet Director had been kidnapped by a wicked genetic engineer."

"I see," translated Bonnie gleefully, "the prince on his dashing white charger rode out to rescue a princess who was the prisoner of an evil enchanter."

"That is what I said," said the Chico. "When Gid arrived at the genetic engineer's dome, he could not get in. The complex was in a force-field."

"The castle was surrounded by a thick thorn hedge," muttered Bonnie.

"Using his trusty laser gun, Gid short-circuited the force-field and entered. Through a small viewing opening high in the dome he could see the beautiful prisoner who had long golden hair wound in spring coils and scanners the colour of copper sulphate."

'Long, fair ringlets and deep blue eyes,' thought Bonnie.

"Gid stopped. Guarding the entry airlock was a huge flame-thrower with fire streaming from its nozzle."

"Oh good, a dragon!" Bonnie told herself.

"Gid had been given a secret formula by a female biologist to make him non-visible. Taking it from the pocket of his life-support suit, he poured it over himself then crept towards the flame-thrower. Its scanners cast from side to side but did not detect Gid. Keeping away from the scorching flames, he sneaked behind it to the entrance airlock."

Bonnie understood that the prince used a magic potion given him by a witch to make himself invisible. The Chico then told her that Gid came face to face with a miniature robot (a dwarf) which he stopped by removing its activating device (turned it to stone), broke the door circuits (picked the lock) and rescued the prisoner.

Outside the dome they met a huge bulldozer (an ogre) which he put out of action with his trusty laser (ran it through with his sword). He turned off the flame-thrower's fuel source (killed the dragon) and escaped with the girl in his moon-buggy.

Both directors were overjoyed to see their children and promised them a planet of their own to direct (their own kingdom) and they all lived happily ever after.

Bonnie thought it was a marvellous story and settled down contentedly to sleep.

It was not long after this, that Bonnie took her exams. The Chico was not allowed into the exam room, so there were no memory banks to help. She tried really hard because she did not want to leave her parents or her beloved Chico and go to school on earth.

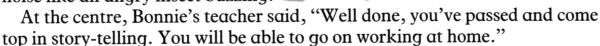

That day, the Chico was behaving strangely, rolling back and forth, whirring and clicking like a person pacing up and down muttering. But that couldn't be – robots are not supposed to have feelings. When Bonnie and her mother went to hear the results and she told the Chico it couldn't come, it made a humming noise like an angry insect buzzing.

At the centre, Bonnie's teacher said, "Well done, you've passed and come top in story-telling. You will be able to go on working at home."

Bonnie was delighted. When her mother asked what her prize-winning story was about Bonnie said, "I wrote the story the Chico told me that night you were held up at work."

When they got back home, Bonnie rushed to tell the Chico the good news. Its circuits whirred and clicked smoothly and contentedly. Bonnie gave it a big hug round its metal waist and said, "I'm so happy, Chico. Thanks to you I shan't have to go away to school. I *do* love you Chico, although I don't suppose your circuits will understand that."

But they obviously did for the Chico said in its metallic voice, "And we shall all live happily ever after!"

Ghost in the Post

Once there was a little girl who loved writing letters. Her name was Kelly. One day, Kelly wrote a letter to her granny in London. She put the letter in an envelope. Then she trotted down to the pillar box at the end of the street.

Kelly popped the letter in the box. Suddenly she heard a loud giggle. Something in the box muttered. Kelly's letter popped out of the box again.

Kelly stared. The letter had been torn open. Was someone playing a joke on her?

Carefully, she looked round the pillar box. There was no one there.

Kelly picked up her letter and pushed it through the slot again. This time the pillar box growled. Then it spat the letter out.

Kelly gasped. Someone, or something, had crumpled her beautiful letter into a messy ball.

Just then old Mrs Bicks came along. "Excuse me, dear," she said to Kelly. "I have a bill to send."

Mrs Bicks dropped her bill in the box. But the bill leapt back out and hit her right on the nose.

Mrs Bicks' face turned a bright purple. "Is this your idea of a joke?" she asked Kelly.

Kelly tried to explain.

Mrs Bicks picked up her bill and jammed it straight down the pillar box. Then she covered the slot with her shopping bag.

The pillar box growled fiercely. Suddenly Mrs Bicks was pushed back. Her bill floated out of the box in a hundred tiny pieces.

"I'm going straight to the police," Mrs Bicks yelled.

Kelly was rather scared. Suppose the police thought she had been playing tricks on Mrs Bicks . . .

Kelly stood on tiptoe.

"Hello," she whispered into the pillar box. "Is there anyone in there?"

"Go away," a tiny voice growled back.

"Who are you?" Kelly asked.

"Never you mind," snapped the voice. "Just drop your letter in and clear off."

"My letter wasn't meant for you," Kelly complained.

The voice in the box giggled. Then it went silent. No matter how much Kelly begged, it wouldn't speak again. Kelly took her letter back home for her mum to post. There were no other pillar boxes where Kelly lived except the one on the main street. Kelly was not allowed to use that box.

That evening a policeman came to see Kelly and her mum. Kelly told him all about the voice in the pillar box.

The policeman wrote everything down in his notebook. But he didn't look as if he believed Kelly's story.

"Mrs Bicks didn't see anyone," he said. "And neither did the postman when he opened the box."

That night Kelly couldn't go to sleep. She was sure she'd heard a little voice in the box, even though the postman had seen nothing. Maybe it was a ghost. Kelly wondered what a ghost would be doing in a pillar box.

Next day, on her way to school Kelly passed by the pillar box again. There was no one around. Kelly put her lunchbox on the ground and whispered, "Hello," into the slot. And then she asked, "Are you a ghost?"

"Of course I am," replied the voice. "How else could I get in here without opening the door?"

"Why are you living in a pillar box?" Kelly said.

"Because no one ever sent me a letter at my old haunted home," came the reply.

Just then Mr Rose the postman came down the road.

"Good morning," Kelly said.

"Good morning," said Mr Rose. He covered the pillar box with a sack and fumbled in his mail bag for a piece of string.

"What are you doing?" Kelly asked.

"I'm shutting this box off," said Mr Rose. "It's no use posting letters in it."

"But there's no other box for miles," Kelly cried.

"Tell that to the joker who's messing around with it," Mr Rose said.

"I will," Kelly decided.

Quickly she scribbled a letter and posted it. Mr Rose tied the sack round the pillar box. Then Kelly went to school.

That evening Kelly laid the toy table in her room for tea. She put sweets on the plates and lemonade in the teapot.

At half past six there was a knock on her window.

"Hello," Kelly said.

A little ghost with a bobble hat on his head floated into the room.

"Thanks for the invitation," he said cheerfully.

Kelly felt a bit frightened but she offered the ghost some sweets and poured lemonade into the cups.

102

The ghost ate and drank politely. "It's a pity you never came to play with me in the haunted house," he said.

"Children are not allowed to go into empty houses," Kelly answered. "But if you promise to leave the letterbox and go back home I'll invite you to tea every Tuesday."

The ghost looked delighted. "That would be nice," he said.

"It would be nice for the people on the street to be able to use their pillar box, too," Kelly said.

The ghost drank up his lemonade. Then he and Kelly played blow-football until bedtime. When the moon shone through the clouds, the ghost floated out of the window and disappeared into the night.

The next day Kelly wrote another letter to her grandma in London. Then she wrote a poem to her aunt in Australia. Finally Kelly wrote a thank-you note to the ghost in the haunted house.

When the letters were finished, Kelly went to see the postman.

"There's no need to worry any more, Mr Rose."

Mr Rose took the sack off the pillar box. And Kelly stood on tiptoe and dropped her letters inside, one by one – plop, plop, plop.

The letters didn't come sailing out again!

Ambrose Pipkin and the Cloth-Eared King

Mr Pipkin the printer had just one son, called Ambrose. He hoped Ambrose would follow him into the printing trade, but Ambrose had other ideas. He dreamed of being a world-famous violinist.

"Whoever heard of a world-famous violinist with inky fingers?" said Ambrose. "I'm off to the big city to make my fortune."

He rented a small house in the poorest part of the city. Every day he practised on his violin. It sounded like cats screeching. Some people ran away with their hands over their ears if they saw him coming.

"I shall start at the top," decided Ambrose. "If I play at the Royal Palace, then everyone will come knocking on my door."

He recorded a tape of his dreadful scraping and sent it to the King.

King Carlo was a great music lover. He opened the tape box eagerly. After two ear-splitting minutes, King Carlo hurled the tape across the room. Then he picked it up again.

"Perhaps we could use this to frighten the rats away in the Royal granary," he said.

But the Royal granary keeper threatened to resign. Indeed, he even offered to sit up at night and frighten the rats personally.

Ambrose was downcast when the postman brought back his rejected tape.

"This shows that the King is a real music lover," bawled the postman rudely through the letterbox.

"King Carlo has got cloth-ears," Ambrose shouted angrily, and he let the flap of the letterbox snap back on the postman's nose.

One day Ambrose caught sight of a poster in the market place.

WORLD-FAMOUS VIOLINIST
BRILLIANT SUCCESSES IN EVERY COUNTRY
RAVE REVIEWS
PERFORMING BY ROYAL COMMAND TONIGHT

These posters were all over the city.

'So, the King has asked him to play at the palace,' thought Ambrose. 'Just because this poster says he's brilliant. How does that cloth-eared King know whether he's any good or not?''

Then Ambrose had an idea. He had thought of a way to pay back King Carlo.

Mr Pipkin was delighted to see his son again. And thrilled when Ambrose asked to use the printing machine.

Four hours later Ambrose came out of the printing shop, looking very inky and staggering under the weight of a big pile of posters.

Mr Pipkin read the top one.

MAESTRO AMBROSIO
WORLD-FAMOUS VIOLINIST
HUGE SUCCESSES ON EVERY CONTINENT
FULL HOUSES EVERYWHERE
(Emperors a speciality)

"I didn't know you were so famous, son."

"I'm not," said Ambrose. "But I've a little matter to settle with the King."

"The King!" Mr Pipkin was impressed.

Maestro Ambrosio's posters went up on every street corner. Naturally King Carlo came to hear about this world-famous violinist and invited him to the palace to give a concert.

Ambrose could hardly wait for the day of the concert. He dressed in his best clothes, and before he set out, he did a very strange thing. He removed all the strings from his violin.

The Court was assembled in the music room, and as Ambrose stepped on to the platform, King Carlo stood up.

"Maestro Ambrosio needs no introduction," said the King and he went on for another five minutes about Ambrose's successes in every country of the world. The information had come from the posters, plus a bit the King made up.

The courtiers began to nod off.

At last, the King sat down.

Ambrose lifted his bow and began a number of sweeping flourishes across the strings. Or rather where the strings had been before he removed them.

"It's a bit quiet, isn't it?" muttered the King to himself.

Then Ambrose began to play what was obviously a slow, gentle melody. He swayed from side to side, dipped and swooped dramatically and closed his eyes, lost in the beauty of the music.

King Carlo waggled his fingers in his ears. Surely he wasn't going deaf? He looked round anxiously. All the courtiers were asleep. Well, that usually happened at these concerts, and they had had a big dinner.

King Carlo tried concentrating harder. He moved three rows nearer to the

platform. He rolled up a programme to use it as an ear trumpet. It was no good.

Whether Maestro Ambrosio was playing gently and sweetly or fast and furious, it was the same. King Carlo couldn't hear a note.

"No, no,' thought the King. There must be some mistake. After all this was Maestro Ambrosio who had played before the crowned heads of the world (Emperors a speciality). Of course he was brilliant. It must be my ears.'

With a wild, final gesture Ambrose swept the bow towards the ceiling, and stamped his foot.

The courtiers woke up with a start. It was obviously all over. Hastily they began to clap and cheer, for they had very good manners. Shouts of "Bravo!" and "More, more!" echoed round the room.

King Carlo looked in astonishment at the roomful of cheering, clapping people. He could hear them all right. So perhaps there was nothing wrong with his ears. On the other hand, he hadn't heard a note of music, and the rest of the Court seemed to have enjoyed it.

He turned to the Court Treasurer and said in some confusion, "Give Maestro Ambrosio a bag of gold, no, two bags of gold. He won't be coming back. I mean, he'll probably be too busy to come back, won't he? Better make it three."

Then King Carlo hurried away to his own chamber, saying he must lie down as he was not feeling very well.

Maestro Ambrosio thanked the Court for their kind attention, refused to play an encore, and made his escape from the Palace as fast as he could.

He paused only once – to toss his stringless violin into the moat where it bobbed about under the window of King Carlo's darkened room for several days.

The Thing that lived under the Bed

Billy dragged his feet getting ready for bed,
He slipped his red jumper off over his head;
His old, blue t-shirt went into the box
Ready for washing along with his socks.
His mother came in and she kissed him goodnight,
Tucked him in snugly and turned out the light;
The door closed behind her and he was alone,
With *The Thing that lived under the bed*.

He took a deep breath and peeked down beneath
And saw two red eyes and perhaps some sharp teeth;
Although it was dark and he'd hurried his look,
He was sure it was evil, this monster, this spook.
It would wait until Billy was soundly asleep,
Then out from the darkness below it would creep
To hunt for the bits sticking out of the sheet,
This *Thing that lived under the bed*.

It could be a dragon with big slimy feet,
Huffing and puffing and bellowing heat;
Which came out at night to snip off some hair,
To take it away to soften its lair.
A lair where it took and kept little boys,
Cleaned out their ears and broke all their toys
And generally did lots of horrible things;
A *dragon lived under the bed*?

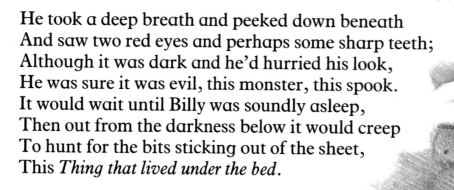

Maybe a monster with a long, pointy nose,
That snuffled around and nibbled your toes.
Perhaps an alien all dripping with goo,
He'd ruin mum's carpet, Oh, what should he do?
On the chair near his bed was an old yellow towel,
He threw it below and then heard . . . a GROWL!
He got such a fright that he shouted out, "Dad!
There's *a Thing living under my bed!*"

Billy's Dad came straight in, "Why are you awake?
Screaming like that didn't half make me shake!
Now what is the problem? You go back to sleep!"
But Billy explained and said, "Dad, take a peep."
Billy's Dad gave a smile then bent down to peer,
Then looked up quite shocked, saying, "What have we here?
Something hairy and growly with a black shiny nose!
A TEDDY *lives under your bed!*"

Billy picked up Big Teddy and gave him a hug,
His father went out, he was feeling quite smug.
Billy ruffled up Teddy's warm, friendly fur
And pressed the small button that made him go, 'grrrr'.
"Thanks, Teddy!" said Billy, "You really are good,
Without you I'd be just a monster's pet food.
You were brave and fearless to stand up and fight
The *Thing that lives under the bed.*"

So every night Teddy is given a hug,
And settled down on the old sheepskin rug,
To watch as the darkness comes over the room
Billy doesn't mind night-time with all of its gloom.
For Teddy is ready whenever the need
To fight back the monster that's out for a feed.
Yes, Teddy is braver and stronger by far
Than *The Thing that lives under the bed!*

Sandcastles Under the Sea

Shaun was on the beach with his grandfather, his grandmother and his big sister, Emily.

His grandfather was sitting in a bright orange deckchair. He was snoring. Zzzz. A large, white handkerchief covered his hot, red face. When he snored, the handkerchief went up and down. Psssh. Up and down. Psssh.

His grandmother was knitting. Click, click, click went her knitting needles.

Shaun's big sister, Emily, was sitting on the sand, slapping sun oil on her arms and legs. Slip - slap, slip - slap.

It was hot on the beach. The sea was bright blue. The sun was like an orange in the sky.

"Will you play with me, Grandad?" asked Shaun.

"In a minute," replied his grandfather. The large white handkerchief went up and down. Psssh. Up and down. Psssh.

"Go and build a sandcastle," said his grandfather. Shaun built a sandcastle. He put a red flag on top and dug a moat around it.

"Will you play with me, Gran?" asked Shaun.

"In a minute," replied his grandmother. She went on knitting. Click, click, click went her needles.

"Go and collect some shells in your bucket," said his grandmother.

Shaun collected plain shells, patterned shells and crinkly-edged shells. He collected shells that were pearly smooth when he ran his fingers inside.

"Will you play with me, Emily?" Shaun asked his big sister.

"In a minute," replied Emily. She went on slapping sun oil on her arms and legs. Slip - slap, slip - slap.

"Go and paddle in the sea," said Emily.

Shaun was hot. The sand burned under his toes. He was tired, too.

'I would just like to curl up on the sand and go to sleep,' he thought.

Shaun paddled in the bright, blue sea. The water was cool and refreshing.

He swam deep down under the bright blue sea. Down, down, down. Down to where the sea was dark blue. Down to where the sea was glassy green. Down to where the sea was shining gold.

Shaun saw a lady swimming in the shining gold water. She had long hair and a long tail.

"You're a mermaid," said Shaun.

"Yes," smiled the mermaid.

"I like your long hair," said Shaun. "I like the little crabs tangled up in it and that orange starfish perched above your ear."

"Thank you," said the mermaid and she swished her long tail.

"I like your long tail, too," said Shaun.

The mermaid smiled again.

"Will you play with me?" Shaun asked.

"Yes," said the mermaid and she laughed. The sound of her laughter bubbled and gurgled up through the sea.

They swam together, up and down, in and out and over and under. The water swirled about them as fish darted by. They tried to catch the fish with their hands but they slipped between their fingers.

They searched for shells. Plain shells, patterned shells, crinkly-edged shells and shells that were pearly smooth when they ran their fingers inside.

They played hide and seek amongst the rocks. The seaweed wrapped itself about them. Shiny, slimy seaweed. The fish watched pop-eyed with popping mouths.

Shaun and the mermaid held hands and swam deeper into the golden water.

"Look," said the mermaid and she pointed a long, white finger.

Shaun saw a large black shape, silent and mysterious. He saw that it was a ship lying on its side, its mast stretched out and broken. A galleon.

"This is where I live," said the mermaid. They swam over to the ship and Shaun saw that the mermaid had hung strings of shells on seaweed over the sides of the ship. They hung in loops like large daisy-chains.

"Come on," said the mermaid and she took Shaun's hand. She showed him the name on the side of the galleon. It was a little faded but Shaun could read it. He traced 'Silver Lady' with his finger. He touched the loops of shells and they were crusty-edged beneath his hands.

They swam deeper down into the ship. The mermaid showed Shaun a large box. She lifted the lid slowly. Shaun saw necklaces of gold and silver, bracelets of diamonds and swords encrusted with precious jewels. The mermaid drew out a long necklace of emeralds and hung it about her neck. The emeralds glinted green and spat out splinters of light into the gold sea. The fishes swam about them and watched pop-eyed with popping mouths.

Shaun and the mermaid left the ship. They made sandcastles on the bottom of the sea. Tall, yellow sandcastles with tall, yellow turrets. The fish swam in and out of the windows and the doors.

Then Shaun and the mermaid swam slowly up to the top of the sea. Up through the gold water. Up through the glassy green water. Up through the dark blue water. Up to the bright blue water at the top of the sea. The mermaid's long hair streamed out behind them. Little waves danced on the bright blue sea, like crinkle-edged bits of lace.

They rode the sea-horses. The sea-horses leapt and leapt again. Shaun and the mermaid laughed with joy and the sound of their laughter rose and mingled

with the cries of the gulls above. The wind blew across their bare skins, like a cool finger stroking. The sun wasn't like an orange now. It was like a squashed peach, its juice streaking the sky crimson, pink, purple and gold.

"Time to go," said the mermaid. She took the orange starfish perched above her ear and gave it to Shaun.

"Time to go," said Shaun. He paddled back towards the beach.

"Time to go," said Shaun's grandfather. He packed away his large white handkerchief.

"Time to go," said Shaun's grandmother. She packed away her knitting.

"Time to go," said Shaun's big sister, Emily. She packed away her sun oil.

"Have you had a nice game, dear?" asked Shaun's grandmother.

"Yes, thank you," replied Shaun. "I've been playing with a mermaid."

"That's nice," said his grandmother.

Shaun turned and waved to the mermaid. She lifted a long, white arm and waved back. Then she dived under the bright blue water. Her long hair streamed out behind her and her silver-sequinned tail swished, then disappeared.

Shaun knelt down on the sand and carefully put his orange starfish into a bucket of sea water to take home.

Wanted: A Kitten

Mr. Grimswade, who ran the village shop, read the postcard carefully. He looked over the top of his glasses at the little girl who had written it. "Do you want me to put this up for you, Samantha?"

"Yes please," said Samantha, and she handed over her money.

Mr. Grimswade took the postcard and fixed it firmly to the shop window. Then he smiled at Samantha.

"That'll stay there a week. I hope you're successful."

Samantha felt very proud when she read her notice, although she already knew it off by heart. Carefully written, in different coloured felt pens to give a rainbow effect, it read:

WANTED:
A KITTEN WHO WILL BE LOVED AND GIVEN
A GOOD HOME.
Apply – Samantha Jones (aged nine) Apple Cottage.

All Samantha had to do now, was go home and wait as patiently as she could.

As she walked home she thought about how much she wanted a pet to love and play with. Mum had said that if she promised to look after it herself, she could have a cat. As Samantha didn't know anyone who had a litter of kittens, she thought of the postcard. She hoped someone would want a home for a kitten.

She was lucky. At teatime that day, there was a knock on the door and as Mum was busy in the kitchen, Samantha answered. On the doorstep stood a tall, thin woman dressed in black with dark glittering eyes and a fierce expression. Samantha stepped back, a little bit scared.

"Are you Samantha Jones, aged nine?" asked the woman.

Samantha gulped and nodded.

"Here," said the woman delving into the basket on her arm and taking out a small, black kitten. "Is this what you want?"

Samantha smiled with delight as she took the little creature into her arms. It was black with bright blue eyes, four white paws and a snowy star on its chest.

"Isn't he beautiful," said Samantha cuddling the kitten happily. "How much do you want for him?"

The woman laughed, a harsh, cackling sound. "There's no charge. I'm only too pleased to get rid of him."

"Thank you, thank you," cried Samantha, but the woman wasn't waiting to be thanked. She hurried down the path as if she wanted to get away before Samantha could change her mind.

Samantha buried her face in the kitten's soft fur and hugged him.

"I shall call you Star-Bright," she said and the kitten began to purr.

Star-Bright settled into Apple Cottage in no time at all. At bedtime, Samantha took him up to her room and made him a cosy nest in her old doll's cot which she placed close to her bed. She loved him dearly and couldn't remember when she had been so happy. She fell asleep with her hand on the little furry body, feeling the vibration of his purr under her hand.

In the middle of the night, Samantha woke up with the moon-light streaming in through the window. Star-Bright was sitting on the windowsill washing one of his little white paws.

"So you're awake now," he said.

Samantha couldn't believe her ears. She thought the kitten had spoken. She looked at him in amazement.

"Yes, yes, I can talk like you, but only at night."

"But, but, but . . . How?" gasped Samantha.

"Look, why do you think the witch was so keen to get rid of me?"

"Witch?" said Samantha. "No, I must be dreaming."

"Pay attention," said the kitten. "You are not dreaming. My mother is the witch's cat and knows a lot of magic. She had three kittens. My two sisters are ordinary cats – the sort that catch mice and sit by the fire, but I take after my mother and I can do magic. The witch thought two magic cats was unlucky so she decided to give me away – that's how you got me."

Samantha was amazed. "What sort of magic can you do?"

Star-Bright had started washing another paw. "Oh, broom-stick riding, spells for weather, charming warts – things like that." He sounded very pleased with himself and rather superior.

"I'd like to see you ride a broomstick," Samantha said.

"Let's go downstairs and find one," the kitten replied.

Samantha's mother kept her brooms and dusters in a little cupboard in the hall. They crept down stairs and Samantha got out the broom. Star-Bright walked round it three times, his tail waving while he muttered some words, then he sat on the end of the broom and said, "Alley-oop!"

The broom stayed where it was but an old umbrella lifted itself out of the hall-stand and started moving round the hall.

Samantha tried not to laugh.

"Beezel-bown," said Star-Bright crossly and the umbrella stopped and lay flat on the floor. "I must have got the words a bit muddled," Star-Bright said. "Do you want to ride on the umbrella?"

"Why not?" said Samantha, so the kitten said the words again. This time, the umbrella stayed where it was while the broom lifted off the floor and began to travel round the hall in a series of jerks.

"Beezel-bown," said the kitten and the broom stopped.

Star-Bright began to cry. Samantha hurried over to him and picked him up and stroked him. "What's the matter?" she asked.

"I was sure I knew the right words and I wanted to show you how clever I was. I've got my spells mixed up and now you won't love me any more."

"Don't cry," said Samantha soothingly. She put the broom and the umbrella away and carried Star-Bright back to her room and let him snuggle down in bed beside her. "Of course I'll love you whether you can do magic or not. It's a terrific bonus you being able to talk. Think of the wonderful conversations we can have at night."

The kitten started to purr. "Well, I am very young. My magic may get better as I get older, then we can go broomstick riding."

"Of course we can," agreed Samantha but secretly she hoped he would forget his spells and just be her friend. She liked him better when he needed comforting than when he was clever and bossy. Anyway, if anyone saw them broomstick riding it might lead to awkward questions.

"I love you, Star-Bright," she said. But the kitten, worn out with his exciting day and his attempts at magic, was fast asleep.

The Green Fairy Dog

Long, long ago when people still believed in magic, fairy dogs lived in the highlands of Scotland. In those days, fairies were spiteful creatures who stole human babies and enticed people into the hollow hills, where, if they ate one bite of fairy food, they would be slaves to the fairies forever. Good, honest folk avoided the fairies.

Fairy dogs were large hounds with green shaggy coats. Their ears were red like a fox's coat as it runs through the bracken. Their eyes were the silvery colour of moonbeams and their sight was so sharp they could see the wind. Men dreaded meeting them for if a fairy dog got near enough to bark three times, the hearer would die within three days.

Angus was a shepherd who tended his sheep on the moors in all kinds of weather. He had a well-trained dog called Shep with a rough brown coat and bright eyes. He understood all Angus's signals and could round up a hundred sheep in no time at all.

In Autumn, Angus brought his flock down from the hill to a sheepfold beside his house every night. At this time of year vixens would go onto the moors to teach their cubs to hunt down unwary birds and straggling sheep. One evening Shep was rounding up the flock while Angus counted them. When the last one was safely in the sheepfold, he looked round for Shep but did not see him. 'Ah well,' thought Angus. 'He will be in when he's hungry.'

Angus was tired and cold – there was a sharp nip in the evening air. He walked to his cottage thinking hungrily of the broth warming on the stove. He went in and closed the door and made the fire burn up brightly. No sooner had he taken the first sip of his steaming broth than there was a gentle scratching at the door. 'Shep,' he thought. 'Home at last and as hungry and cold as his master.' Angus poured broth into Shep's bowl, lifted the latch and opened the door.

The night outside was very dark. Angus, blinded by the firelight, couldn't see the dog but he knew he must be there.

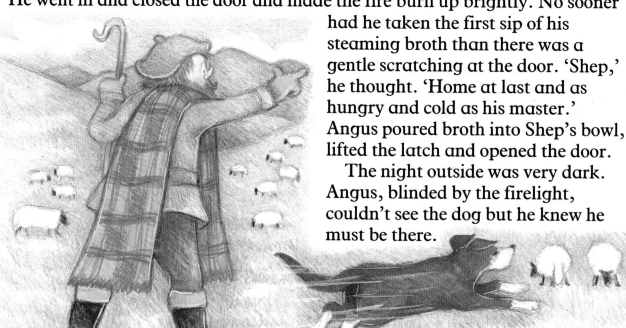

"Come in," he said impatiently. But it was not Shep who brushed past him. It was a larger dog with a greeny-grey coat, red-coloured ears and strange, light eyes. The hair on the back of Angus's neck lifted as he realised it was a fairy dog. He longed to push it out but by the laws of hospitality he couldn't – he had invited it in. Had it come to foretell his death? He did not think so, for the look in its silvery eyes was gentle and it had made no sound, let alone barked three times.

With trembling hands Angus offered the dog Shep's bowl of broth, but the fairy dog went to Shep's bowl of clear, spring water instead. It lowered its great head, lapped a little and then settled down by the fire with a sigh. Warily Angus sat in his chair and began to drink his broth.

Again there came a scratch at the door. This must be Shep. Angus rose to let him in. Shep stopped on the threshold, sniffing the air. When he realised what kind of dog had taken his place he laid back his ears and whimpered. Belly to the floor he crept underneath Angus's chair. As Angus watched, he saw to his amazement, the fairy dog push Shep's bowl towards him as if to bid him to drink.

After a while Shep overcame his fear enough to sup his broth but all night he stayed beneath Angus's chair where Angus sat, not feeling it right to leave the dogs while he went to bed.

123

When at last daylight came, the fairy dog rose, stretched and yawned. Gently he licked Angus's hand; his soft, pink tongue felt as light as a moth's wing against his palm. The dog walked to the door and as soon as Angus opened it, the dog disappeared into the morning mist.

For several nights after that, Angus was wary when Shep scratched to come in but it was always his own dog outside the door and gradually he forgot the fairy dog.

When winter came, the weather got colder and Angus wrapped himself more tightly in his plaid to keep out the knife-like winds. Late one afternoon snow started to fall, huge flakes dropping thickly onto the hillside where it filled the hollows in which the sheep were sheltering, huddled together for warmth. Angus knew he must gather them quickly and get them home before they were buried and frozen to death.

He whistled to Shep to herd the flock while he probed the hollows with his crook for missing sheep. While Shep was digging out an old ewe trapped in a flinty hollow, he gashed his leg on a sharp stone. Angus found the dog whimpering with pain while the white snow round him was dyed red with his blood.

Angus tore a strip from his plaid to bind up Shep's leg. The snow was falling fast now, like feathers from a burst pillow. The light was going and Shep could not work with a wounded leg.

Angus couldn't possibly find all the sheep himself before darkness closed in; he could get some of them home but many would be left in the snowdrifts to freeze.

To Angus the loss of his sheep would mean poverty and sorrow – he loved his flock but more than his sheep he loved Shep and although the gallant dog was trying to work, limping on three feet, Angus would not have it and picked him up to carry him home.

Suddenly there was a tug at his plaid. He turned and saw the green coat, the red ears and the moonbeam eyes of the fairy dog. Gently the huge animal nuzzled Shep then swift as the wind, began to search out the sheep, doing Shep's work. The green-coated dog ran swiftly and tirelessly, seeking the buried sheep, digging them out, herding them towards Angus and soon, he gathered the whole flock. Then, with Angus carrying Shep in the lead and the fairy dog at their heels behind, all Angus's sheep were safely herded into the pen and bedded down for the night.

Angus opened the cottage door and said to the fairy dog, "Come in," but the great, gentle hound shook its head and put its warm tongue into Angus's hand as if to say, 'farewell' and vanished into the snowy night. It was as if the dog had been waiting for a chance to repay the shepherd for his hospitality and having done so, was satisfied.

Angus never did see the fairy dog again but he never ceased to be grateful to it for saving his flock on that winter night and he would never allow anyone to speak ill of fairy dogs in his presence.